DEVIOUS SAVIOR

VICIOUS VIPERS MC 6

LYNN BURKE

DEVIOUS SAVIOR

I was responsible for my soulmate's death, and twenty years later, the demons of guilt still try to suffocate me. Drowning them with liquor doesn't work, so I run, leaving everything—my colors, my brothers, and my addictions behind.

Fate brings me to a place that matches my dried out soul—Vegas.

A ray of pole-dancing sunshine breaks through my darkness, giving me hope for a future. An independent, stubborn woman, Casey doesn't need me to be her knight in shining armor, but I can't give up my addiction to her.

She's an inescapable temptation. A curvy glass of thirst-quenching water. And she's off limits, under the protection of the Vegas Chapter.

When Casey's life is placed in my hands, will my lies and her manipulation be our undoing or will facing our insecurities save us both?

DEDICATION

For my lovie, Ivy

CONTENTS

$$1$$

RICKY

A big-ass sign above the highway caught my eye, its four arrows telling me where I headed.

Las Vegas. City of sin.

I'd toured almost every damn state east of Nevada in my attempts to bury the demons of my past.

Cold had been creeping into New England when I'd hightailed it out of there after tossing my colors on Vigil's desk, but desert heat swarmed the cab of my truck. My open windows allowed the rush of wind to fill my ears and mess my too-long hair, but it sure as fuck didn't lessen the warmth seeping straight into my brittle bones. I'd left the ocean far behind, but the landscape stretching as far as the eye could see matched my heart a thousand times better. Dried up, incapable of life beyond the prickly, scraggly sort.

Had my subconscious brought me to the desert knowing it's where I belonged?

For twenty years, my emotions had attempted to suffocate me on a daily basis. I'd tried to drown them with liquor in return. Passing out created a blackness where I didn't feel those fucking demons, a void I imagined death would be like.

No conscious.

Darkness and fucking peace.

But the ugly truth had always resurfaced at the crack of an eyelid—or sometimes with nightmares so vivid, I would see her face again, bluish-purple and slack, vomit in a pool around her blonde hair. Waking to those memories only made the demons howl louder like shrieking banshees looking for a soul to devour.

I'd lost my own soul on that day. I'd also lost the only person who adored me to the point of reverence. Addiction. She'd needed me in ways no one on the goddamn planet did. I was her savior, her world. She was mine.

Until she no longer drew breath ... because of me.

It should have been me.

Teeth clenched against that familiar demon's whisper, I sped down the highway, looking for a place to crash for the night.

I fucking paid the price for my own addiction all those years ago, losing the love of my life. Initially, I'd gotten clean, but seeing my Viper brothers finding their old ladies the previous couple of years had twisted my insides straight to hell with grief and guilt. Whiskey had become my girl, oblivion my mistress. I'd gone back to my old ways of lying to cover my stupid ass when I'd been too drunk to function, but I hadn't fooled a damn soul.

Vigil's ultimatum of getting clean once and for all or getting out was the shove I'd needed to get my head set on straight again, but rather than stick around with the only family I had, I'd lit out like that damn banshee nipped at my heels. I'd emptied my apartment above the Vipers' club. I'd cleaned out my bank account. Up and left my one-man subcontracting electrician business. I stuffed all my shit into the cab of my truck and in bins around the bike in the bed, and I'd taken off westward, New England in my rearview mirror.

With no rhyme or reason, I'd travelled highway after highway without a clear destination in mind, seeing the sights and passing out fucking sober as shit in a different hotel every night. But with each mile that stretched between me and my past, the pressure in my head had lessened. My emotions quieted enough I no longer fought to drown them as they did to me.

I'd gone through the usual withdrawals from slugging down too much whiskey like I had while attempting rehab in the past, but by the time I'd crossed into Nevada, I breathed a bit easier. Didn't crave a bottle. I'd been sober for over four weeks, not a damn drop of alcohol finding its way past my lips. Longest I'd ever gone.

I'd become a tonic man. Lemonade when I needed something with life, more of a kick. Sucking down a cold pink one especially reminded me of my childhood before bad decisions and resulting guilt took to eating away at my head.

Vegas reminded me of the sweet tartness of my youth. The city rose like robust life amidst the arid land beyond its limits. Buildings jutting from rock and dust, people seemingly everywhere even though it had to be close to ninety degrees beneath the baking sun.

I finally took an exit, pulling into the first hotel I ran across. Standing in the parking lot, overnight bag in hand, and the noise of traffic like static in my ears, some part of me settled even though I didn't care for noise and crowds. Almost like I'd found ... home. Why not settle in Vegas for a while? See which way the hot as fuck wind blew? At least the heat was dry and didn't drip sweat down my t-shirt even with the lack of a breeze.

Although I still had a decent nest egg cash-wise and enough investments to last me a couple years of the nomad life, I needed to keep my hands busy and my thoughts occupied.

I slid my key card in the room's lock.

Maybe I'll check out the classifieds...

"Ricky Capone!" A deep voice hollered.

I jerked around, dropped my bag, and reached for the gun in the back of my jeans on instinct, barely managing to keep from pulling it out in broad fucking daylight.

A big as fuck black man strode toward me along the sidewalk, shades hiding his eyes, but I recognized the size and beard on the man, never mind the leather cut he wore. We'd met at Sturgis years earlier. Klingon, Vicious Vipers MC president of the Vegas chapter.

"Klingon." I tucked my gun away, thankful as

fuck I hadn't needed to pull it fully out to protect my ass.

"The fuck you been, man? Your brother is worried sick." Klingon clasped my hand and pulled me into a bro hug. Even at my six-foot-two height, the fucker towered over me. "Why the fuck haven't you called—and why the fuck you in my town without my knowing?"

He stepped back, shoving his shades atop his head, and I picked up my bag from where I'd dropped it beside me. "Just got into town," I said, lifting it for him to see. "Been traveling all over the country. Landed here."

"You sticking around or just passing through?"

"Was thinking about staying for a while. Vigil tell you why I left?"

Klingon nodded while studying my face. "Why don't you come over to the club tonight after you get settled in?" he asked, his voice lowering. "We've got some dumb fuck a few doors down who needs to have his face rearranged. Maybe lose a few fingers or toes. You're welcome to join in the fun."

"Club shit?" I asked, wondering why he even considered including me in their business. If he knew why I left the east coast, he knew I was no longer a Viper.

Another study of my face lasted a few seconds before he nodded. "Got some young punks moving in from L.A. thinking they can take over our territory."

"Bikers?"

"Nah. Stupid fucks who wear their pants down around their damn thighs. Bandana fuckers. So, you gonna come over tonight, or what?"

"I handed in my colors," I reminded him, that fact spoken out loud lancing an ache through my chest. I attempted to ignore it along with the other regrets in my life. I missed the club life, the comradery, and feeling of belonging—but I knew I'd made the right choice in leaving.

"Don't give a fuck you aren't wearing your cut," Klingon said, blunt as fuck, no nonsense.

"I'm not a Viper anymore."

"Did you disrespect your colors?"

"Just left them on Vigil's desk where he'd find them."

"Dues paid up to date?"

I eyed him, wondering where the fuck he was going with the questioning. "Yeah, but I've missed too many meetings."

Klingon shrugged like all that shit didn't matter.

"So, pay the fines. Vigil isn't going to kick you out. He wants you home."

I shifted, glancing down the empty sidewalk along the motel's front. "I disrespected the club too many times. The brothers won't ever trust me again."

The feel of Klingon's stare pulled my focus back to his stern face. "I think they'd make an exception considering your past."

"I'm yellow," I bit out, hating to voice the truth of my weakness.

"The fuck you are. I've heard the stories. You're one badass one-percenter—just got personal shit to deal with." He shrugged. "We all got it. Everyone deals with their shit differently."

"I'm not going back." That fact I knew clear as fuck.

"Then transfer here. Tell you what." He glanced over his shoulder from the way he'd approached. "We're having a BBQ tomorrow afternoon at the club." Meeting my gaze head on, he put on his *I'm in charge* face. "If you're hanging in my town, I want you around as a guest at least. Stay, don't stay, your fucking call, but we're going to get caught up since Sturgis last year."

Klingon was a man used to being obeyed, and even though I knew his officers and club probably wouldn't appreciate his bringing me into the fold when I'd left my colors back in Boston, I found I didn't want to turn his offer down to be a guest.

"Sure thing."

"Good." His intense stare lightened. "Now, go call your brother and let him know you're not in some shallow grave or swimming with those damn fishies out in the Atlantic while I clean up this mess."

"Shit went down back there?" I asked, knowing as the president of the Vipers he knew I asked about lost life.

"Not yet—but it will." He glanced down at my bag. "You packing?"

"Always."

"Still a good shot?"

"Best brother back east."

He grinned, his teeth flashing in the sunlight. "So, you *do* consider yourself a Viper."

My brow furrowed over my word choice calling myself a brother. "Habit."

"Tomorrow. Three o'clock. Be there, or I'll kick your ass." Klingon spun and stalked off, and I turned once more to unlock my door. "Call your brother!" he hollered over his shoulder. "Fucker calls me just about every other day asking if I've seen or heard from your ass."

"Will do," I promised even though I still wasn't ready to.

Klingon paused and turned. "You know he claimed that woman and her son?"

"Michelle?"

"Mila."

My brow furrowed as I fought to recall the woman in his neighborhood I'd heard he'd gotten tangled up with. But I'd been drunk more often than not those final weeks before leaving. "Thought her name was Michelle."

"Yeah. So did he." Klingon chuckled. "Think it's time you called home, boy."

I huffed a snort through my nose. *Boy.* Klingon couldn't have more than a year or two on my thirty-nine, same as my brother. "Yeah, I'll get right on that shit."

"You're a bad, goddamn liar, you know that?" he hollered for everyone within a dozen or so yards to hear.

Yeah, I knew it. Been a devious fucker my whole life—from mischievous childhood to addict who always had a cover story. "I'll let him know I'm alive."

"Good." Klingon's firm tone returned, and he nodded. "He deserves that much, at least."

I lifted a hand for a quick wave.

"Tomorrow!" he hollered, and I nodded.

Guess I'm gonna stick around for a while.

That thought drove me to check out the classi-fieds, online and old-school style in the newspaper once I settled into a room. Finding a few contractors looking for electricians, the decision to stay solidi-fied in my head.

I set up a couple appointments for the following week.

Long after I made the calls, I sat in my hotel room's lone chair, staring at my brother's contact information on my cell. I'd fucked up before leaving. Still dealt with a ton of shit—jealousy and bitterness at the top of that fucking stack when it came to my older brother. Insecurity being the bottom-most level from which it all shot upward to fuel those emotions I'd been running from.

Not ready to listen to him chew me a new asshole, I grabbed my boots and shoved my feet back into them. I'd told Klingon I would contact Vigil, but I didn't say when. Keys in hand, I locked up my hotel room and walked the two blocks through the early evening toward the bar advertising titties and lap dancing I'd passed on the way in.

Not that I was on the prowl for pussy. My fist had been fine the past month on the rare occasion I woke up with a hard dick, but I needed something other than my own fucked-up life to think on.

For the first time in ages, a hint of hope lit inside me—a new fucking life, maybe a new beginning far from my demons of the past. Maybe they'd eventually keel over and fucking die. That thought had me wanting to celebrate in some small way, so why not enjoy some flashing titties and maybe some pussy?

I sat in a corner, thumping bass filling my ears, flashing lights focused on the stage where two women fucked poles in nothing more than G-strings filled my vision. My dick lay bored alongside my thigh. I'd expected my mouth to water at least for a strong drink, but nothing.

Fucking nada. In some ways, that was a good fucking thing.

Confident in my decision to avoid the liquor I could smell in the air through cloying perfume and sweat, I settled back in my chair, hands on my thighs, waiting for a woman to spark some life into my limp dick.

"What can I get ya?" A leggy brunette in a mini skirt and corset flashed a smile, checking me out from my auburn-ish hair to jeans in need of a washing machine. At least I'd showered and used deodorant. Hadn't sunk that fucking low since giving up the bottle.

As with the rest of the women loitering around, she didn't do jack shit for me.

"Lemonade?" I heard myself ask.

Her lips twitched. "Seriously?"

"Just a tonic," I replied a little gruffer than necessary.

"Tonic."

"Yeah—Pepsi, Coke, whatever you got."

She nodded and left me alone, same as every woman who got what they wanted from me. Not that *I* wanted anything more. It's why I'd stuck to the club whores back home, sharing them more often than not with Devil since a third wheel always kept emotions to a minimum. The whores knew I wasn't on the market so hadn't bothered trying. Didn't stop them from spreading their legs or dropping to their knees, though.

Drink in front of me, I pulled out my cell and stared at Vigil's name as song after song blared overhead, swiping the screen to life whenever it went black. I didn't look up once since my first glimpse of the brunette did nothing for me.

Contacting Vigil would open the door for him to start tossing out demands. Orders for me to get my ass home. Being the nosy fucker he was, he would ask a million questions, and I would be tempted to spew lies and shit even though I no longer needed to.

Bad fucking habit.

But Vigil was my brother, the only living blood I had. And Klingon had been right—he deserved to know I lived. Fuck knew he'd had my back every day since I'd been born regardless of my fuck-ups—and the sins we shared. Even his ultimatum had been for my own good. Hadn't realized it at the time, but I'd done a shit ton of soul-searching in the previous four weeks.

One deep inhale, and I forced my fingers to text out a message. **I'm in Vegas. Been sober for a month.**

Three dots started blinking seconds after I hit send.

Vigil: **You okay?**

No cursing, no trying to set me straight or order barking... I'll admit my own eyebrows hitched up even while that lancing ache speared my chest again. He'd always been concerned for my wellbeing, but fucking insecurity had always made me expect the worst when it came to him.

Me: **I will be.**

Vigil: **Thank fuck. I'm here, brother. I'll always have your back.**

Five minutes passed without a question or order to return home. It must have been hard as fuck for him to not order me back home, but Vigil gave me what I needed. Space to breathe. Time to maybe kick my demons' asses since all his attempts to help had failed.

Me: **Thanks brother.**

The screech of a guitar whined, drawing my focus up to the stage. My breath oomphed right out of my goddamn lungs like a kick of black exhaust, and my heart stalled out.

A perfect fucking mirror image of my love before I'd fucked up and lost her...

Petite blonde. She had curves for days, yet lithe with muscle, the good bits covered by scraps of virginal, white lace. Long blonde curls framed a heart-shaped face, blue eyes heavily painted. And those full lips ... red and puffed like she'd been sucking dick for an hour straight.

My nightmare flashed in my mind, and I blinked, fighting to do away with the image of the woman who haunted me from the grave. My chest felt like a dozen knives plunged in deep, twisting and jerking, to ruin me all over again as my heart fought to beat.

Fuck.

I sat frozen. Staring and unable to look away, drinking in the sight of the tiny dancer. She pranced with a brazen confidence that my love never had. She sassed the patrons with every toss of her hair and sly smirk while gyrating and bending, contorting her body like only a limber gymnast or ballerina could.

It's not her.

My dick swelled regardless of the wave of grief that caught me up in agony. Demons battled against my body's instantaneous need. Regrets quickly overrun by lust.

The dancer turned my way, and although I doubted she could make me out clearly in the darkened corner, her lips parted and cheeks flushed. Her attention drifted toward me more often than not while she dry-humped the pole with those bits of material covering what any sane man would want to peel off.

That smirk. Those eyes narrowed in a siren's gaze. The angling of her body, the holding of her perfect tits in offering my way, their plump ridges smooshed together, begging to be fucked. Nipples tight as fuck beneath the lace she didn't peel off her body.

And when she bent clear over, peering at me from between her spread legs, a darkened spot on that scrap of lace promised she felt what I did. Her long hair brushed against the stage's floor, and I imagined the strands in a fall of blonde waves around my face as she rode me straight to fucking heaven.

Goddamn. All woman in a small package, a fire cracker if I'd ever seen one. More Vigil's type than mine personality-wise, but he'd found his old lady, Klingon had said.

I'd wanted a happily ever after once, but with the shy girl who had clung to me as though I was her reason for living, her trusting me to provide for her and see to her safety. I'd failed on that last part in a big fucking way.

The desire for liquor slammed into me, but I clenched my teeth and waved over my waitress, needing more of a distraction. *It's not her*, I told myself—but I needed to know. Needed to see her up close. Touch, fucking feel the tiny dancer wasn't my Annie. "Manager around?"

"Yeah, I'll get him."

Blondie held me entranced, and I barely spared the guy a glance when he loomed over me. "How much for lap dance?" I asked, motioning at the stage with my chin.

"Casey doesn't do private dances."

Casey...

I pulled two hundreds off my wad of cash from my pocket and lifted them toward him. "Ask her if she'll do it just this once."

"She's off limits."

I finally gave him my attention, cash still held out in offering. "Yours?"

Dark brow furrowed, he glanced at her. "No."

"Then ask."

Lips in a tight line, he took the bills while eyeing the others in my palm and nodded, pocketing the money as he moved off.

No woman had caught my eye since I'd lost the love of my life, but Casey sure as fuck had. Because she looked a lot like Annie? Didn't fucking know, but a driving force to see her up close, look into her eyes, and find she wasn't *her*, would have gladly pulled more bills from me if the manager had hesitated any longer and given into his obvious lust for cash.

Awareness of her shivered over my skin, and I swear to fucking God Casey winked at me before sauntering backstage. Sassy little vixen.

Definitely not my Annie.

2

CASEY

His eyes...

Intense and blue, even from the corner he hid in, the man's gaze pierced the lounge's haze of salivating males, the loud music, and the cat calls. All noise faded when our eyes connected. My breath and pulse sounded loud in my ears, like everything muffled to only what truly mattered—a connection of two souls.

So damn fine.

I might have bent a little lower. I definitely gyrated against the pole and ran my hands over my body while imagining him doing so. Taking my focus off him to turn and smirk at other horn balls salivating over me created a sense of guilt even though I'd always loved the attention.

I'd never seen that blue-eyed babe before, and I couldn't keep from watching him watch me. For the first time since I'd started dancing for money, a man's stare turned me on. And stare, he did, soaking the bit of lace covering my pussy clear through.

Did he notice when I bent and shook my ass his way? Did he imagine shoving his gorgeous face between my cheeks and eating me out until I lost my voice from screaming—because I sure as hell couldn't help but fantasize about that very thing.

I didn't strip like most of the other dancers did, but I felt as though he could see clear through my lace coverings, his intense gaze caressing every inch of my skin.

Shit balls, the man turned me on. I even winked at him before slipping backstage.

My boss, the club's manager Skin Tight, met me in the back hall, his brow furrowed like trouble brewed.

"What's going on?" I asked, breathless as hell— and not from dancing. Even my nipples ached, rivaling the throbbing between my thighs.

"Guy out there wants a private dance."

My jaw damn near hit the floor, and I blinked, wondering why the hell Skin Tight even approached me. "You know the rules, ST."

"Yeah, but he pulled out two hundreds like they were pennies—and he had a pile of them in hand."

I crossed my arms and eyed my boss. He'd agreed to let me dance without stripping because I was damn good at it, but my father was the real driving force behind getting me my job—same as everything else I felt got handed to me.

While thoroughly independent to a fault, there were times I did enjoying having a father the locals feared, rightfully so. The only two humans in the world who got to see his softer side was his only daughter and the woman he'd been madly in love with for over thirty years.

"Who is it?" I asked, knowing my father would be shaking his head with a resounding *no*, a death glint in his eye for my even considering a private dance.

"Guy in the corner. From the east coast—has a Boston accent."

"Blue eyes? Tight dark t-shirt?" *So damn fine my panties are a soaked mess?*

Skin Tight's lips pressed in a thin line, and he nodded.

"I'll do it," I rushed to say, suddenly breathless again, my pulse racing.

"But your father—"

I rested my hand on Skin Tight's chest, shutting off his train of thought. "Just this once," I whispered, leaning in so the dancer approaching from the dressing room wouldn't hear—not that anyone but my boss and I knew who I really was. "I won't tell if you won't. And, it's 50-50 split or no deal."

His gaze narrowed again. "You could probably weasel another hundred or two. He seemed pretty determined to get what he wants."

"I'll keep that in mind." I winked. Men never crossed my father. Ever. Skin Tight had some serious balls on him. But, he did love cash... "Room one open?"

"Two is—and I'll keep the cameras on just to be safe."

I nodded and patted his chest before dropping my hand. "Send him in there. I'll freshen up a bit and see how much more he's willing to pay for an up close and personal dance."

"Your father is going to murder me," he muttered, turning away.

"I can keep a secret if you can!" I whispered loudly, unable to hide my smirk. Skin Tight and his love of crisp hundred dollar bills. I'd seen what my father had handed over in order to get me the job I wanted since I hadn't been able to land the coveted dancing position at one of the casinos.

It had paid off, too. Skin Tight's crowd loved me, and I made more dancing on a weekend than all those uppity bitches in their feathered costumes up on fancy-assed stages.

Win-win. At least that's what the bitter part of me told myself.

At least I was doing what I loved since my other dream had come to a stalled-out halt. Pushing those thoughts aside, I dabbed a little powder on my face to do away with the shine, sniffed my armpits to ensure I hadn't sweated too badly, and decided to skip the panty change I'd planned on.

Still wet and ready for more, I snuck down the hallway toward room two.

My man with the intense blue eyes sat on the chair in the middle of the room seemingly relaxed with his hands on his jeans-clad thighs. The tension rippled off him, sending a shiver of goose bumps along my skin as he drank me in the second I clicked the door shut behind me.

I held still, hand on my hip and a smirk on my face, allowing him his eyeful while I took one of my own in the setting-the-mood dim lighting from overhead.

Longer blondish-auburn hair hung over his brow, in desperate need of a cut, and gold glinted in the short beard along his strong jawline. Bedroom eyes women swooned over studied me from head to toe before settling on my face.

"Come here," he ordered, his ragged, low voice pebbling my nipples to hard points.

While I wasn't one to follow orders without a fight, I moved closer, adding an extra bit of sway to my hips, slinking forward in my fuck-me heels with confidence. I'd never done a private dance before. Wasn't even sure how to approach him or where to begin without music drowning my scattered thoughts, but I wanted it. Wanted him. Period.

Gaze glued to mine, he held out a hand, and I entwined my fingers through his, palms clasped. Energy rippled through me, parting my lips, and catching my breath. I knew what drowning meant in that moment.

Gone to the world, caught up in desire so potent, I wanted to throw myself at his feet and beg.

Casey Dawes didn't beg, though.

His focus slipped to our hands for a moment, a furrow flitting over his brow as though he felt the connection I did—and didn't like it.

"What's your name, stranger?" I asked, not yet

ready for him to take off as his tensed body suggested he considered doing.

"Ricky." He glanced up at my face again, his sky blue eyes unshuttered in a way that flooded me with all sorts of feels.

"I'm Casey." Although tension still strung me tight, I moved in, straddling his thighs, our clasped hands twisting behind my back—his doing. He smelled like soap and old leather. Talk about butterflies taking to flight.

Rock hard thighs flexed beneath mine, shifting me closer to his chest. "That your real name?" he asked.

"Yeah," I whispered, sounding like a needy whore—I loved it. I eased closer still, settling against a rock of another sort. Fuck, the man had to be aching, straining against my pussy like he did. I ran my hand along his whiskered jaw, and his eyes closed briefly, allowing my touch. Up over his ear, into his hair ... I tangled my fingers enough he opened his eyes. A gyration of my hips clenched his jaw, but he moved with me. "New to town?"

He swallowed and nodded, his focus dropping to my lips.

I licked my lower lip hoping to entice him and ground against his groin, sparks shooting off straight from my clit bumping against the back of his hard length.

"You're not her."

His quiet declaration caught me off guard, breaking the smooth rhythm of my hips taking me close to the edge of an orgasm. He touched my lower lip with his thumb, rubbing softly back and forth over the wetness I'd left behind.

I stilled. Couldn't move beyond breathing as he stared at my mouth as though entranced. His eyes weren't cold like the men I'd grown up around. Vulnerability shone through, like a window into his soul. Pain rolled off him, furrowing his brow, but he lifted his attention to my eyes once more, searching my face, memorizing what lay a mere foot away from his.

"You're not her," he repeated on a whisper, and the pain etched on his face brought out my empathy big time.

"I'm not." I cupped his cheek again, his whiskers tickling my palm.

One more swallow, and he focused on my mouth again, his thumb still resting on my chin. He tugged, parting my lips.

"I want to kiss you, Casey."

My heart thumped heavily in my chest, all

compassion for his pain scattered to the ends of the earth. *Fuck, yes.*

"So kiss me, Ricky." I'd gone for sassy siren, but sounded like a needy whore in my own ears.

"Sorry..." He leaned in and claimed my mouth before my mind registered his apology—and all thought flitted away immediately after.

I'd kissed my fair share of men—without my father knowing, of course—but I'd never been consumed. Ricky stole my breath, took control of my thrumming pulse, every swipe of his lips melted me against his rock-hard chest.

A shuddering sigh ripped through me, and I allowed him entrance to my mouth, whimpering with every stroke of his tongue against mine.

I've never truly been kissed before.

That thought hit my brain loud and clear. Our mouths together were more than a touch of flesh—it felt more like a life-giving force, something I knew I would crave the rest of my damn life, and the way our bodies moved together, mimicking fucking...

Shit balls.

I was a goner for a complete stranger from the other side of the damn country. An ache so damn sweet, so potent rose from my core, soaking through my panties enough to wet his jeans.

My hips moved on their own, chasing what his flexing ass and thrusting tongue promised.

I detonated, shuddering through my climax, grasping at his hair, his mouth swallowing my cries.

Lord above have mercy, because Ricky owned me. One touch, one kiss, and I *knew*. Mom had always told me that's how it would happen...

One last shiver over my skin, one last whimper, and I loosed my hold on his hair, my other arm still tightly banded behind me as he held me tight, his entire body trembling beneath me. I pulled back, blinking back to reality, my ears ringing.

Warmth shone through the lust in his eyes, and he literally gulped as he focused on my face. He blinked, and an invisible shroud seemed to settle down over him, chilling my skin.

"Ricky?" I whispered as a sense of distance settled between us with the icy coldness in his eyes.

He grasped my upper arms, setting me on my feet, and stood, hands fisting at his sides.

I tilted my head back—really far back—to keep my focus on his profile. Strong nose. Perfect lips, so damn soft and delicious.

He stood like a statue, unmoving and frigid, his focus on the door behind me. Death-like silence hung between us, the thrumming of my pulse the only noise in my ears.

I touched his fisted hand, and he strode around me without a word, the door snicking shut quietly behind him before I could open my mouth to beg him to stay.

A totally different type of ache took over the sweet one still tingling between my thighs, and I sank into the chair we'd shared, the warmth of his body lingering. Arms wrapped around myself and knees drawn up, I stared at the closed door wondering what the hell had just happened.

Ricky was the type of man I always felt myself drawn to. Emotionally needy and yet a gentleman. I'd heard all kinds of horror stories of private lap dances the other girls got paid for, but Ricky had kept his hands to himself other than devouring my lips. Hell, he'd even told me he wanted to kiss me before doing so, almost as if he was asking permission.

Shivers pebbled my skin again, and I touched my lower lip.

Wherever the hell my hot as fuck stranger had come from, I knew two things for sure: He knew how to kiss me senseless, and he was the honorable type my father would approve of.

Determination to find out who Ricky was rose quick and strong. As my father's daughter, I knew how to get what I wanted, but I wouldn't be using him or his connections to find my man.

My man.

I couldn't help the smirk that tilted my lips. A hint of a tribal tattoo had peeked beneath his t-shirt along his bicep—and I wanted my name there in scripted ink as well.

Property of Casey Dawes.

"Fuck, yes."

Once more in control of my faculties, I scrambled off the chair and went in search of Ricky, but he'd gone from the club. Jaw set, I changed and went to see Skin Tight for my hundred dollar bill and to see what else he knew about the stranger from Boston.

3
———

RICKY

The little dancer left a wet mark on my jeans, and I'll admit to taking them off the second I got in my hotel room and sniffing her musk deeply into my starved lungs. I fucked my fist right there, back against the door as guilt ate at my soul, filling my fist with spunk.

Casey sure as fuck wasn't my Annie—far from it—but she'd taken over my goddamn head. Her sweet as peaches scent. Her satiny skin. Her warm breath caressing my lips. The gentle touch of her palm on my cheek and the tightening of her fingers in my hair... Fucking siren bent on wrecking my goddamn brain.

Guilt over forgetting Annie in that moment had made me set Casey aside, and I cursed myself fifty times over after getting back to my hotel. Why the fuck I didn't just bury myself in her tight heat beat the hell out of me. She'd sure as fuck wanted my dick. The fuck was wrong with me?

Fucking guilt. I couldn't allow myself one goddamn minute of enjoying life.

I showered, a scowl set on my face. Jerked off with my damn jeans to my nose again, fantasizing about fucking Casey's little pussy raw, then dealing with a double load of feelings as though I betrayed the memory of my old lover.

I slept like shit, Casey's sultry pout and blue eyes replacing the usual nightmares, so I couldn't exactly complain.

My gut told me to head back to the strip joint and find out who the hell she was, where she lived, and how soon I could get into her bed. My heart told me it was better to avoid love than to fuck up again and lose it. My head assured me the connection we'd felt couldn't be trusted even though it overshadowed anything I'd felt in the past—even with Annie.

But I didn't deserve to be happy.

That thought ringing in my ears, I hit a barber shop a few blocks down from my hotel to waste time on Saturday morning. I felt human again once the mop atop my head sported its usual fade and my beard clipped close to my jawline.

I wasted more time by doing a full body-weight workout right there in my room, same as I'd been doing in every hotel every night. The endorphins left after killing myself always gave me a sense of satisfaction. Seeing the muscles cut beneath my skin gave me a bit of confidence my sorry ass had always lacked.

Vigil was jacked. Had been since seventeen or thereabouts. I'd always been a step behind—

I cut the thoughts off and focused on my workout, not quitting until I needed a gallon of water to rehydrate my ass.

Two hours later, I headed west toward the Vegas Viper's club, my stomach in twisted knots. I wasn't exactly in the mood for company, but Klingon had demanded my presence, and sitting in the hotel room waiting for the next two days to pass until Monday when I was set to meet with a contractor wasn't wise. I'd either end up salivating for liquor or fantasize about Casey enough my fist fucked my dick raw.

"Fuck," I muttered, adjusting my swelling length while exiting the highway. Fucking girl...

I wondered if she danced on Saturday nights, too.

I told myself it didn't matter since I had no desire to love another woman or connect with another soul. But fuck if my dick and heart didn't war it out with the rest of me. Fucking emotions of a different sort trying to drown me.

Goddamn my life to hell.

The second I parked in the Vipers' lot, my scowl eased. Unlike the club back home, the Vegas chapter didn't have an enclosed compound. The place sprawled out more like a shopping plaza, single story, dozens of bikes lined up along the front. A parking area off to the left showed as many if not more trucks and cars.

One hell of a party...

Three o'clock on the damn nose, and Klingon stood out front, bottle of beer in hand as though waiting for me.

He clasped me tight against him again, slapping my back like I was the prodigal son returned home. "Good to have you here, brother."

I didn't correct him calling me a brother, but found myself grinning for the first time in months. "Good to be here." I meant it, too. Fuck, I missed affection. Hadn't realized exactly how much.

"You talk to Vigil like I told you to?" he asked while stepping back.

"Texted him. Told him I'm sober and in Vegas."

Lips tight and dark eyes studying my face, he nodded. "He tell you to get your ass back home?"

"Surprisingly, no."

Klingon flashed his teeth. "For the best if you ask me. Come on. Party's around back."

I followed him around the side of the sprawling building, fighting off the desire to shove my hands into my pockets. I'd never been a people person like Vigil, but with my choice to settle in Vegas for a time, I figured it wouldn't hurt to have a friend or two—if any of the Vegas Chapter chose to see me as more than a disloyal bastard, unworthy of trust.

With one-percenters, the club came first. Above family. Above old ladies. Above personal fucking problems of which I had plenty. Leaving my colors behind had been the right thing to do since I'd been a serious fuck up who couldn't do the job I'd been appointed to, but if Klingon's men found out, they'd probably see me as a traitor.

Maybe I'd made a mistake accepting Klingon's invite. I actually had fucking butterflies as we rounded the building.

Holy fuck...

Talk about a fucking crowd. The hot sun beat down on dozens of old ladies, brothers in cuts, and youngsters up the ass. The Vipers' club had to outnumber ours by thirty at the least. A shrieking kid ran past, another on his heels, water balloons fisted in each hand. I side-stepped to keep from getting plowed into, actually chuckling at their antics—but it could have been my nerves.

A huge pit grill roasted racks of chicken, and a few grills smoked, lacing the hot air with the scent of burgers. Two big tables sat laden with food like everyone had brought a dish to share, and I hunkered back into my skin, my smile fading. Showing up empty handed ... Auntie Jeanie had taught me better than that.

"Shoulda brought something," I muttered as Klingon bent to squeak open a cooler at the crowd's edge.

"Don't worry about it." He tossed me a can of pink lemonade of all things and cracked himself a beer. "You're staying sober as fuck, right?"

"Yeah." Fuck, the man was intuitive as shit, just like Ryker had always claimed about his childhood friend.

"I know why you left home." He captured my

focus and held it, his dark eyes searching deep—fucking shrink if ever I'd seen one. "I had demons of my own back in Boston. It's why I left the east coast and ended up out here, far from Southie where Ryker and I grew up. I got my shit together. Became a new man." He paused to study me for another minute, and I let him see whatever he would, determined to be vulnerable and learn from others who went through shit and made it out better on the other side.

"I see hunger for the same thing in your eyes, Ricky."

My throat tightened, and I nodded. "New start. New life."

He clasped my shoulder and grinned. "Glad to hear it, and there's plenty of that shit if you want more." Klingon clinked his beer against my lemonade. A wink, and he tilted his head toward a group of Vipers before sauntering their way. "Got some boys you'll want to meet."

I recognized two of the five Vipers we approached, a quick glance at patches confirming Klingon's Sergeant at Arms and enforcer, neither of whose names I could remember from Sturgis a couple of years prior.

"You boys remember Ricky Capone—VP of the

Boston chapter," Klingon said as we entered their circle.

I should have opened my mouth to correct him, but snapped it shut. Interrupting or correcting an officer would stain my reputation with his brothers before I even had a chance to earn their trust.

"You remember Butcher and Balboa," Klingon said, motioning toward the two I recognized, thank fuck he named them, and I nodded, shaking both their hands. Both stood eye-level to my height, the Sergeant at Arms at least a decade older than me with gray shot through his hair, Balboa a decade younger if not more.

"Don't let Balboa's blond curls and innocent baby blues fool you," Klingon said with a snort. "Young fucker knows how to throw down. Best to avoid pissing him off, Ricky. Wouldn't want to see your pretty face fucked up."

I fucking laughed. *Laughed.* No one had ever called me pretty.

"This is our treasurer, Pennies, so-named because he pinches the fuck out of them."

I eyed the bright, coppery knotted as hell patch atop his head, one eyebrow raising in question. "Hair had nothing to do with that name?"

"Fucking mop helped in that naming, too, yeah."

Pennies rolled his eyes and grinned, or at least I thought he did, his damn beard was so out of control I couldn't see his lips.

"Our secretary Crank," Klingon pointed out the oldest by far of the group with a full head of gray hair and a beer gut hanging out over his low-slung jeans. "He's our head mechanic. And that short bastard is Prophet, our VP."

Prophet was short as fuck amidst the rest of us, but his wide shoulders and hammer-like fists suggested he knew how to have a brother's back. I remembered hearing he'd had Stone's and Ryker's when the two had come out to Vegas a few years earlier to steal Stone's woman back from the fuckers who'd planned to sell her as a sex slave.

I shook his hand. "Heard you like guns," I said, and he nodded.

"Ex-marine. Sniper."

"Kinda of fond of them myself—there any good shooting ranges around here?" I asked.

"Plenty. Maybe a couple of us brothers can head out there soon and see swhat you're made of," Prophet said with a grin.

"I'd like that." No lie or half-truth in that statement.

"So what brings you to Vegas?" Butcher asked, his cool gaze taking in my lack of a cut.

"Needed a change of scenery." Not exactly a lie, but far from the fucking truth, too.

"I remember you were drunk off your ass every damn day in Sturgis last year."

I forced a grin. "Isn't that what Sturgis is all about? Whiskey and pussy?"

Two of the brothers chuckled and lifted their beers, but Butcher didn't so much as twitch an eyelash, his attention riveted on me. As the Sergeant at Arms, I didn't expect anything less. He finally dropped his focus to the sweating can in my hand.

"Gave it up?"

I nodded.

"Leave the boy alone, Butcher," Klingon said, his tone gruff, and Butcher finally turned away from me. "We're going to need him for that little issue we've got going on."

My eyebrows shot up, and a quick glance around the group revealed a bunch of closed lips and wary eyes.

"He's not a member of the Vegas chapter," Butcher said through grit teeth.

"Ricky Capone is the fucking VP of the Boston chapter. He knows what we do, how we make our money. He's got the goods on us to put us all away if he wanted—but he's not that kind of man. He's loyal."

"He left," Butcher stated without looking at me— like I wasn't right the fuck there.

"And he has his reasons," Klingon said, angling to face his brother better. "Same as I did."

"You didn't leave behind a club and your colors.'"

"And Ricky didn't come here looking for new ones. It was my idea to bring him in as a guest. I'm going to talk to Vigil about a transfer—if that's what Ricky wants. And if he does, I want him and his guns with us for the take down in two weeks."

"Why's that?"

"Because he's good with those fucking things. Has a steady hand and no remorse."

Again, I had to clench my teeth to keep from interrupting the two officers, but for more reason than I didn't see myself as a patched member to any club. No remorse, he'd said. I held remorse over one lost life even though I hadn't pulled the trigger. But did I want to patch in with the Vegas brothers? I thought I'd left that lifestyle behind. Planned on becoming a different man—a better one. Could I move forward wearing the Vipers' colors, or would I end up face planting again?

"I don't like it," Butcher said, still ignoring my presence while I stood there, feeling the other officers' stares.

"You don't like anything but your old lady and daughter, you grumpy fuck," Klingon muttered. "Ricky's my guest for today. Don't like it, take a fucking hike." He turned to face the rest of his men while I fought to keep from shoving my free hand into my pocket. "Any of you other fuckers have a problem with my friend being here today?"

I glanced around too, my stomach twisted up fucking tight. Everyone shook their heads, but I still felt like I shouldn't have accepted the invite. Didn't fucking belong...

Someone hollered the food was ready, and our group disbanded. Balboa, the enforcer I'd met the year before, went out of his way to slap my back as Butcher stalked off. "Ignore the prickly poppa bear. Glad to have you here, brother."

"Let's grab some burgers," Klingon grumbled, rubbing his gut. "I'm fucking starved."

I followed along, shaking hands with brothers he introduced me to on the way to the grill. The chicken had my mouth watering, so I detoured off on my own, Klingon's, "Make yourself at home," spurring me onward toward the open BBQ pit rather than the grills where he headed.

A couple of old ladies dished out the food, and I didn't have one goddamn complaint over my first plate full of homemade foods outside a damn restaurant in four months. Dozens of picnic tables strewn across the dusty ground, and a quick glance around had my feet pointed in Klingon's direction where he sat with a couple of patched brothers—not including Butcher, thank fuck.

Couldn't blame the man for watching over his club, though. I wouldn't have liked having my ass there either if I was him.

Klingon slapped the bench beside him in offering, a burger with one huge-assed bite taken out of it, his jaw going. "Ricky Capone," he introduced me to the table after swallowing. "Brother from Boston."

"Pleased to meet you," I muttered a good six times over to the men crowding the table, letting the "brother" thing slide again out of respect. I dug into the chicken and potato salad, filling my stomach until I couldn't fucking breathe.

Once finished, I pushed aside my plate and leaned my arms on the table, a slight smile on my face while listening to the brothers banter and tell crude jokes. No one showed interest in digging into my story like Butcher had. Whether they took the lead of their president or just didn't give a fuck, I didn't care. Kept me from having to toss out half-truths again.

A kid's squeal drew my focus toward the club, and like a goddamn sledge hammer hit me square in the chest, my breath left in a rush.

Casey.

The squealing little boy launched himself at her as she approached the party, and she laughed, her face shining and eyes bright as she caught him up in a hug. I couldn't hear a word Casey said, but her lips moved with animation, the laugher and joy in her eyes like fucking *life*.

Two other kids raced to her side, and she knelt to hug them tight, ruffling hair and tweaking noses, all three sets of youngsters' arms flailing like they told stories, vying for her attention as she straightened once more. Casey threw her head back and laughed, the sunlight glinting off her golden curls, and the sweetest goddamn ache spread through my chest.

Light *and* life.

She lit my dark world like a spotlight in the blackest night, dispelling every goddamn shadow and demon from my head. My focus glued to her, my hands itching to touch, my mouth drooling like mad to taste her sweetness again.

But what the fuck was she doing at the Vipers MC?

Club whore.

"Fuck." A scowl dented my brow at the sudden thought, and my stuffed-full stomach cramped.

"What?" Klingon asked, and I tore my focus off Casey.

She was a dancer at a strip club—even if she hadn't stripped those little bits of lace off her body. What else could she be than a club whore, used ten times over by all the unclaimed brothers littered around the lawn?

Fuck.

Klingon glanced toward where I'd been staring and turned back toward me. "You know Casey?" he asked.

I glanced up again—couldn't fucking help myself —but lied with a shake of my head while clutching my lemonade can in my fist to the point it dented beneath my grip.

"She's Butcher's daughter."

Fuck. Me.

My heart fell for a whole different reason even

though I was happy as fuck she wasn't a club whore. Still off-limits, even if I *was* interested.

I couldn't help but stare again, my feet itching to take me to her as she greeted her father with a warm hug, head tilted back to laugh up at him. He smiled down at her like she was the light of his life, too.

Definitely off-limits, I told myself, a grim as fuck hardness settling in my gut. There was no fucking way her father would want her anywhere near me.

I also bet he didn't know she danced for dollar bills ... but I sure as fuck wasn't going to rat her ass out.

Slugging down the last of my warm drink, I grimaced.

Casey isn't my type.

I'd said that very thing in my head at least ten times since she'd creamed all over my jeans the night before. She was too outgoing. Too confident, too vocal, and cocky. I bet she didn't feel the need for a man, didn't crave his affection, his attention in the way I longed for a woman to do with me.

Fuck knew she got enough from her parents and the kids running around, never mind the brothers and other women who made their way over to greet her.

Casey was the queen, the Vicious Vipers MC her

court, and hold it, she did. Well. Warmly greeting every single person with a smile, some with hugs, and others with laughter, her father not far behind —like a goddamn poppa bear.

I sank further into my shell, the husk of the man I'd once been, and I forced my focus off her.

Klingon clasped my shoulder. "You okay, brother?"

"Yeah," I managed and forced a grin, lying through my fucking teeth.

Didn't matter she was off limits and I told myself she wasn't my type—I fucking wanted her like the desert surrounding us thirsted for raindrops from the bright blue sky overhead.

4

———

CASEY

It was nice to be back at the club, seeing the little ones who'd grown in the six months since I'd last stopped by. Usually, I sat and read books or played games with the kids, acting the big sister quite a few of them didn't have. The love I got in return? Priceless. Even after months of being caught up in my own world, the kids remembered me and filled my heart with love.

A shiver slid over me, similar to the one I'd felt the night before while dancing for my man, and my smile faded a bit while I ruffled little Johnny's hair.

I hadn't been able to find out jack shit about Ricky. Nothing. Skin Tight had no clue who he was, nor did he share more than a half dozen words with him to stab a guess beyond Bostonian with his hint of dropping his R's. None of the other dancers I'd spoken with had recognized him. Neither had his waitress who confirmed the slight Boston accent.

Definitely an out of towner passing through, and I feared I was shit out of luck. My heart ached, but I had other contacts I could probe for information, the whole reason I'd decided to show up at the club's yearly fall Vegas-style BBQ.

Hell, who was I kidding? The scent of smoking ribs and chicken lay thick in the air, sending a rush of saliva to coat my tongue.

A shiver slid down my spine, but my daddy approached, a warm smile on his face.

"Pumpkin."

I burrowed myself against his hard chest, the sense of complete safety and unconditional love swarming through me as it always did when he wrapped me in his strong arms.

I leaned back, my smile coming easy. "Hey, Daddy."

"Glad you could make it."

"Been awhile."

He squeezed me again and released me. "Looks like you've been missed." My dad chuckled while taking in the kids swarming around us.

A young couple I recognized, one of the newer

Vipers and his old lady, moved our way, their son on his father's shoulders. If I remembered correctly, the little guy had just turned three.

I held out my arms as they drew close, my squealed, "Evan!" lighting up the toddler's face. Guess six months hadn't been too long, because he came to me like I was his best friend, settling onto my hip after I smothered his cheeks with kisses.

"You're getting too big!"

"Right?" his mom agreed, and leaned in to give me a quick squeeze. "Where've you been?"

"Busy." I focused on Evan, bouncing him up and down on my hip while he blabbered about whatever toddlers did. While Daddy knew I danced at a club, I'd always felt the need to hide the truth from his brothers and the old ladies. I wasn't embarrassed by my profession of choice, but maybe my parents were.

Then again, none of the Vipers ever came to the lounge that I'd ever noticed, and it wasn't like the place was too far to drive if any of them were in the mood for a titty show. I expected my dad hadn't wanted his brothers ogling me and declared Skin Tight's place off limits.

"How's school going?"

I let out a sigh, my smile less bright. I'd applied to UNLV School of Medicine for the fall term, but my mediocre grades hadn't been enough to get me in. With my bachelor's degree in biology I'd struggled to earn in May, I could easily land a job in the medical field with a bit more schooling, but my heart had been set on being a pediatrician. I also didn't want to leave Nevada in order to do so.

"Med school is on hold for now," I told Evan's mom, my smile starting to feel forced.

"Everything okay?"

I nodded and kissed Evan's forehead. "Didn't get into UNLV, and I don't want to move too far from home. Still haven't decided what I want to do."

Mom saved the day, finally breaking away from the ladies that must have been holding her hostage since she was usually attached to my dad's hip. She leaned in to kiss me.

"Are you coming for lunch tomorrow, too? It's been weeks," she said, stepping back and smiling at Evan.

"I'll be there." My smile came easier—and that shiver licked down my spine again. The feeling remained while we chatted, but my quick glances around didn't reveal anyone watching me.

Dad moved closer and his and Mom's hands clasped, fingers lacing together as though without thought—same as always when they stood close. A pang in my heart for the same type of love they shared hit me as it had been doing over the previous couple of years. At twenty-six, I was far from becoming an old maid, but no one had snagged my attention in the way I expected one would need to strap me down for good ... until Ricky.

That damn shiver... My pulse shifted into hyper drive, and I took my time scanning the crowd, somehow knowing he was there. I caught sight of Klingon's bad ass at a picnic table, but the profile of the man beside him kicked the butterflies in my stomach to flight.

Heat rushed through me, settling into my cheeks and between my thighs. He'd gotten a haircut and had trimmed his beard since the night before, but it was my man. Even though he didn't look my way, awareness of him swept through me, weakening my knees.

Evan reached for his mom, and I handed him over, trying like hell to not stare and wish Ricky's attention turn toward me even though my mind chanted for him to do that very thing. I wanted —*needed*—his eyes on me. Needed to feel that rush again, those sweet tingles throughout my entire body.

He must have noticed me. There's no way the

awareness of being watched I'd felt earlier had come from anyone *but* him.

Daddy pulled me into a side hug. "Whatcha looking at, Pumpkin?"

I tore my focus off Ricky and grinned. "Not sure yet."

But I knew. Oh, how I knew.

Energy raced over my skin, and every cell in my body screaming *hallelujah, he's looking*, I glanced Ricky's way. Our gazes latched on like salivating pit bulls, refusing to let go, stubbornness and longing entwining in a beautiful dance that lit up my insides.

He was the moon to my night—

"Don't get any ideas," Daddy snipped.

"Hmm?" I asked without looking away from Ricky's intense gaze.

"He's a friend of Klingon's from back east. VP of the Boston chapter, last I'd heard."

Skin Tight had it right...

"And not nearly good enough for you," my dad added before I could open my mouth to toss out a million questions.

I felt Mom's stare on the side of my face as I tore my focus off Ricky to smile up at the protective beast looming over me. "Okay, Daddy." I patted his chest, playing the obedient one as always, but I had every intention of getting to know Ricky regardless of my dad's thoughts or orders.

"I'm serious." He scowled down at me.

"Of course you are." I rose on tiptoes to kiss his cheek, and he lowered his head to allow it. Big softie. I didn't bother biting back my chuckle.

"Come get some food," Mom said, pulling me away from my dad. The second he was out of earshot, Mom whispered, "You'd better be careful."

The pile of ribs called out to me, and I grabbed a plate. "What do you mean?"

"A mom knows—and anyone who saw the way the two of you looked at each other just now would, too."

I glanced over to find my mom's face serious as fuck, but her eyes twinkled.

"How do you know him?" she asked.

Feeling Ricky's continued stare, I couldn't help a quick look in his direction. Shit balls, the man was fine as fuck. And those eyes... "He was at the club last night."

"Mmm."

I turned away and grabbed the tongs lying atop the ribs, ignoring the knowing noise escaping through her nose. "And Daddy has nothing to worry about."

"I'm calling bullshit, Casey."

I couldn't help but laugh while piling ribs on my plate. "Okay ... so I talked Skin Tight into letting me have a private moment with Ricky."

"Shit, girl, you're asking for trouble," she muttered under her breath. "And?"

"And nothing. We kissed, he set me aside, and took off like I'd left third-degree burns on him. Know anything about him? Does Daddy?"

"I haven't seen him before today, and I've never heard your father mention him."

I nodded and finished filling my plate, setting aside the topic of the man I couldn't help but feel with every inch of my body. Even sitting a good twenty or so yards away from one another at separate picnic tables, I could feel every time he looked my way. The desire to say fuck it all and just go plop myself on his lap where I belonged tempted me to the point I decided to press my luck.

Daddy could go suck an egg if me being my usual friendly self offended him.

I left Mom with the others sitting at the picnic table, using the excuse of needing a drink. The cooler closest to us held what I wanted, but I rifled through the ice for a few seconds like I couldn't find what I looked for before letting the lid snap closed, my hands empty.

The next cooler sat closer to Klingon's table, and I made my way toward it, stopping to greet people along the way, my skin on fire the entire time, and not from the sun shining down on my head and shoulders bared by my halter top.

I knelt down beside the cooler, taking my time digging out a can of lemonade.

A shadow fell over me as I'd hoped, and I glanced up to find Ricky's head haloed by the sun. I squinted up at the god who'd graced my dreams the night before, the one whose name crossed my lips when I'd gotten myself off after waking up that morning.

"You look like you could use one," I said, breathless as hell and holding up my drink.

He took the ice-cold can without a word, the heat of his fingers brushing against mine soaking my panties and racing my pulse.

I stood and tabbed open another can of lemonade, my focus on his eyes, both of us drinking in the sight of the other while wetting our tongues. Had his mouth been as dry as mine?

"Butcher's daughter," he rasped after swallowing the lemonade he'd guzzled, his gaze unwavering and just as intense as the night before while I had imagined he was my dancing pole.

"VP of the Boston chapter," I tossed back with a smirk.

A hint of a frown furrowed his brow at my statement. "Used to be." Ricky finally glanced away. "I handed in my colors a month ago."

A loaded statement, and his face revealed a shit ton of pain—and regret. Before I could think what to say, he met my gaze head on again.

"Does your father know what you do?" he asked quietly.

"Yes."

Ricky's eyebrows jacked up, a quick glance at where I knew my dad sat and I expected watched us.

"He allows me an outlet for my creative side since he knows I'd do it without his blessing anyway." I gave him the easy explanation rather than get into the whole, *I couldn't get a job as a showgirl dancer for the wildly popular Jubilee!-like show that took Vegas by storm the year before and didn't get into med school, either* truth. No one but me needed to know of my failures, my weaknesses. "Besides, the owner is his friend. He looks out for me."

"You're a rebellious one," Ricky murmured, his focus dropping to my mouth, and he didn't sound too thrilled with the description he'd labeled me with.

"Independent," I corrected him even though I *had* been rebellious as a kid. "There's a difference, and my parents love me enough to allow me to make my own choices. They just like to keep reins in the background to keep me safe."

"So that little lap dance last night was a no-no," he whispered, peering into my eyes again as though tempting me to lie.

"Yep."

"Why did you allow it knowing your father wouldn't be pleased? Sounds a lot like rebellion to me."

"I agreed because I wanted to. The draw was—*is* —too strong."

His blue eyes blazed, solidifying the truth in my head. He felt it too.

"I like you," I stated plain and simple, my entire body a live wire as I smirked up at him. "I *want* you."

Ricky blinked, probably surprised by my blunt reply, but I wasn't one to mince words when I knew what I wanted and went for it. He glanced toward where Daddy sat again, and I waited for him to take me up on my offer even though I hadn't exactly made one.

"Not gonna happen, tiny dancer." Ricky clinked his can of lemonade against mine and strode away, leaving my mouth hanging wide open.

Denied. Well, I'll be damned.

I laughed even though I could have sworn a knife twisted through my heart. Ricky, VP of an MC club or not, had to know we belonged together, and even though his inner pit bull had relented, mine sure hadn't.

Come hell or hopefully heaven, I would have him. I would make him mine.

I caught Daddy's eye and he glared. "Sorry," I mouthed, shrugging and biting back my smirk. "Just being friendly."

Forget the egg—Daddy could suck a full dozen of the damn things.

5

RICKY

Fuck, was she beautiful. She was also one hell of a wildcat, and even though I told myself countless times she wasn't my type, I couldn't keep my goddamn eyes off her. As the sun sank, the brothers got a bit louder, the families started to take off for the night, and the music turned up from the outdoor speakers attached to the club's back wall.

Girls started dancing—and I got hard as fucking nails even though Casey didn't shake her ass like she'd done on stage the night before. Twice, Klingon simply stated my name, tearing my focus off her. Lips in a tight line, he shook his head, telling me without words the woman was off limits—as if I didn't fucking know it. I managed to avoid watching her for all of five minutes before the draw became too strong.

The second time the president caught me staring, I decided to call it a night since my body couldn't lie as easily as my lips. I knew it was only a matter of time before Butcher decided to make a scene.

Couldn't have her—both Klingon and her father had made that clear without a goddamn word, but I didn't deserve a second chance or the kind of happiness a woman's attention brought anyway.

I made my rounds saying goodbye, feeling as though I might have made a few friends, and even though Butcher stared me down with a hard glint in his eye, I approached him out of respect. Told myself I was just being friendly, doing the honorable thing seeing as how he was the protector of the club, but I sure as fuck had ulterior motives if I was being honest with myself.

His old lady sat sideways on his lap, leaning against his chest, his hand in a possessive hold on her thigh. That damn twinge I got whenever I was with my brothers and their women back home arched across my pecs, stinging like a thousand hornets.

Fucking sucked.

"It was nice meeting you," I said, offering my hand.

Butcher shook my hand, surprising the hell out of me since I'd caught him watching me eye up his daughter over a dozen times. He didn't say the same, just kept his lips zipped in a grim line.

His wife, however, had a twinkle in her eye. "You, too, Ricky. We hope you'll stick around for a while."

Butcher grunted, not exactly in agreement, and with a nod, I spun away, shoulders hunched and ready for some silence.

I made it all of ten steps around the club before I felt her but I didn't slow, kept right on stalking across the parking lot, my fingertips tingling with the need to touch her satiny skin.

Respect, I told myself, *and it's only your dick that wants her. You can live without.*

"I'm working tonight," Casey said, catching up to my side, breathless and so damn obvious, my dick swelled. The rush of her sweet peach scent swarmed my nose and jerked my dick inside my jeans.

"Have fun," I bit the words out through clenched teeth, forcing myself to keep going and not stop to turn and drink in the sight of her. The longing to just listen to her voice, stand beside her, soaking in her warmth, her enthusiasm for life, knocked my fucking knees.

I didn't expect she'd be dismayed by my lack of interest with how determined of a woman she seemed to be, but she laid off without another word, her footfalls going silent as I left her in the dust.

She didn't even stand where I'd left her when I peeked over my shoulder before climbing into my truck. A part of me was bummed over that fact, but I liked my women demure and shy. Quiet and clingy. Needy for a man to take her under his wing and protect her.

You didn't protect Annie, though, did you?

"Fuck." I broke out into a sweat, my mouth watering for liquor as the memory of her lifeless body flashed through my mind. Eyes clenched shut, I tipped my head back against the headrest and focused on breathing in and out, my hands in a death grip on the steering wheel. Counting slowly until I calmed the fuck down took a hell of a lot longer than usual.

Maybe staying in Vegas wasn't such a good idea. I turned the key in the truck's ignition, but didn't shift into gear. Being on the road, driving all day and then working out in a hotel's gym or doing body weight training in my room had worked to keep me occupied for four weeks. The second I decide to stick around somewhere, all fucking hell broke loose with those damn emotions trying to drown my soul.

All because of one tiny, blonde dancer who resembled the woman I'd been responsible for once upon a time. The one I'd loved and failed.

I went back to the hotel room and did another full body workout, killing my already exhausted quads with squats and chest with pushups until I lay panting on the floor, sweat dripping off my body. Still, I thought of Casey, thought of what I did, yet didn't want.

Talk about a fucking war.

The thought she would be on stage and have to head home by herself in the early morning hours didn't sit well in my gut. She'd brought out my protective nature, something else I hadn't felt since Annie. Not sure how I felt about that fact, I hopped in the shower, knowing I couldn't just turn it the fuck off—even if Casey didn't need my protection with the whole Vegas Vipers MC having her back.

Telling myself I wasn't being a stalker creep, just my usual devious self, I headed back to the strip joint. Skin Tight eyed me as I sat in a dark corner, but didn't approach me. The same waitress from the night before brought me a drink without asking—a tonic.

I'd been warned without words to stay away, but watching and getting up close and personal were two totally fucking different things. Some would call it toeing the line, but I called it staying under the radar. Finding loopholes to fill my eyes since I couldn't fill my hands. Wasn't outright disrespect in my eyes.

Casey waltzed out onto stage an hour later, stealing my breath and my goddamn heart. Our gazes clashed, and the temptation to beg her for five minutes in private and the knowing I didn't deserve the life she offered had me out of my seat and out the goddamn door before her set even ended.

Feeling like a fucking loser, I sat on the edge of my hotel bed, head in my hands. Loneliness pressed against me on all sides. For the first time in twenty years, I wished for a woman to share my personal space. Needing me. Giving me a sense of purpose.

But Casey could never be that girl.

I needed to get her the fuck outta my head.

6

CASEY

Oh, how I wanted to confront my dad. Rip him a new one for warning Ricky off me. Although he'd shown up at the club, he'd lit out before my dance ended. My moves fell flat the second the lounge's door shut behind him, and all joy fled. I continued on, my sexy smirk feigned, and for the first time, dancing became a chore.

The fact he couldn't stay away, though, should have given me a bit of hope, but I knew my daddy. No man crossed him if threatened.

Why else would Ricky deny me? The energy between us could not be reasoned away. The kiss we'd shared...

My pissiness over not achieving my goal followed me to my parents the next day for our weekly luncheon which I'd skipped out of the previous month or so. Body thrummed tight with need, my lips in a thin line, I greeted my dad when he opened the door.

I didn't go as willingly into his arms as usual.

"What's wrong, Pumpkin?"

"Nothing," I bit out.

"Someone bothering you at work?" he asked, holding me at arms' length, his eyes growing cold and distant, a look I knew from my wild days.

I shook my head. "Just a bitch today."

His face relaxed and he chuckled at the line Mom and I always used when we were on the rag— even though I wasn't. "Go grab a drink from your mom. She's got some blue, fruity cocktail made up for the two of you."

In need of a buzzed brain—*relaxed* brain—I did as told.

Mom took one look at my face and handed me the glass of blue fruity shit Daddy had mentioned. She glanced beyond my shoulder, probably to see if he followed me. "Casey?" she asked, turning her focus back on my face.

I took a nice long drink of the sweetened vodka and smacked my lips. "Damn, that's good."

"What's going on?"

Flopping down at the table she'd already set, I shot a scowl toward the living room where my dad must have plunked his ass back into his favorite chair. The sounds of football announcers rose, letting me know I'd guessed right.

"He told Ricky to stay away from me, didn't he?"

Mom leaned against the counter, grabbing up a mitt while glancing at the oven's timer. "He didn't use words this time, but his scowls couldn't be misinterpreted."

"He caught Ricky staring at me." I didn't need to voice a question since I knew that answer already—Ricky hadn't been able to keep his eyes off me all afternoon. There's no way my dad didn't notice.

"Yes."

"And the death glare came out," I muttered, glaring once more at the wall between the kitchen and living room.

"Mmm hmm."

I turned my focus back on Mom and met her gaze head-on, my chin tilting upward. "I want him."

She laughed lightly, her blue eyes twinkling with a knowing look. "I can tell. I think everyone who was at the party yesterday could tell."

The air rushed from my lungs as I slouched in the chair, elbow on the table and chin propped in my palm. "I'm not going to obey him this time, Mom," I said, keeping my voice low. "Not with this one. I need you to help me."

Mom didn't reply, and I felt like a bitch for asking for her to help me get my way. She always deferred to Daddy. Always. It's what kept things running smoothly in their home, I had no doubt. My dad didn't take shit from anyone, even the love of his life.

"I don't know Ricky enough to plead his case," Mom finally answered, and I chewed over ideas as she removed the roast from the oven. "Maybe if you talk to your father, tell him how you feel, he'll lighten up. I'm assuming Ricky ignored you when you hurried after him last night since you returned to the party so quickly?"

"Pretty much," I mumbled. "He showed up at the lounge later, though, and the energy between us even a room away from one another heated me more than the spotlights. Then he took off like his ass was on fire before I even finished. Made the rest of my set a boring chore."

Mom's eyebrow rose as she glanced at me over her shoulder. "Since when is dancing boring?"

"Since Ricky's eyes weren't plastered on me." I got up and helped her dish up the food, my mind running over Saturday evening, same as I'd been doing since trying to pass the fuck out the night before.

"David!" Mom called my dad. "Roast is ready!"

Neither of us said a word until our plates were filled and steaming in front of us.

"So, what do you know about that Ricky guy?" Mom asked, and my heart stuttered.

I cast a quick glance up at my dad to find him eyeing the two of us. "I won't be manipulated, so don't even start."

Huffing out an annoyed exhale, I stabbed a roasted potato. "Is he a danger to me or the club?"

"Not that I'm aware of."

"What's his story? What is it about him that you don't like?" I pushed, needing to know why my dad didn't like him.

"Just a gut feeling, but he left the Boston chapter which shows where his loyalties lie," Daddy muttered and shoved a forkful of gravy-dripping roast into his mouth.

I glared at him while he chewed, and he glared right back in our usual clashing of the stubborn asses whenever we disagreed. "So, you're judging him simply on the fact that he left. The facts surrounding it and his story for doing so doesn't matter."

"It's my gut intuition."

"I need more than that, Daddy," I snipped, knowing my eyes flashed. Having moved out, I no longer feared his wrath. He couldn't take away my cell. Couldn't ground me.

Daddy let out a slow exhale through his nose, loud enough to let us know his exasperation had kicked in. "Ricky Capone has a darkness about him, Casey Lynn. Demons, current or past, hover around him."

"What the hell kind of answer is that?" I shot back, my frown biting deep into my forehead at the use of my first and middle name. "Everyone has regrets and issues in their past. You said yourself it's a man's past that shapes him."

"That kind of haunting pain in a man's eyes promises trouble." Daddy's gaze softened. "I've seen it before. Dealt with enough brothers to know when they're fighting inner battles."

I lifted my chin, and Mom had to know what was coming—I was enough like her and we thought on the same vein. "Maybe he needs a good woman to help him battle those fuckers."

"Casey."

"I'm serious." I stared back at my dad, arms crossed even though I hadn't finished my lunch.

"Mom was your saving grace—you've said it countless times. The two of you never would have happened if Grandpa told her to stay away from *you*. God knows my independent spirit didn't come from her."

Daddy glanced across the table at my mom, his beard twitching in the tell-tale clenching of his jaw.

Oh, I had a couple points, alright, neither of which he could argue.

"He's not good enough for you," Daddy tried the same excuse as the day before, not bothering to glance over at me but going straight back to his food. "I want better for you, Casey. You're going to medical school. You're going to become a pediatrician. Neither of those dreams of yours line up with being a biker's old lady."

"Says who?" I shot back, still acting the petulant child and not giving a shit because my heart continued to ache over not getting into UNLV. "Prophet's wife is a lawyer. She's an upstanding person in our community. Being an old lady doesn't mean one can't be professional."

"Until I know what demons Ricky has on his ass and why he disrespected his colors by leaving them back east, he's off limits."

Bam.

Line set in a tone I knew all-too well. Even Mom cringed and glanced at me, her eyes begging me to obey.

Did I trust my father enough to sniff out Ricky's demons? As the Sergeant at Arms, it was his duty to protect the club, and I didn't doubt he'd have answers to his *gut intuition* before long.

"Will you have time to figure him out, or is he headed back to Boston soon?" I pushed.

"From what Klingon seems to think, Ricky's sticking around for a while."

I nodded, at least a little relieved. But could I wait for Daddy to figure him out? What if Ricky took off before I got a chance to be with him, one-on-one, even if we didn't make it beyond talking? Yes, I wanted his body on top of and beneath mine, just the thought of it soaked my panties, but I wanted to know what caused his pain. What had made him set me aside despite the strong draw we obviously felt toward one another?

Like Mom, I wanted to fix everybody and every-thing. I wanted to hug the hell out of the hurting. I wanted to soothe away the boo boos from children and adults alike. Couldn't help myself. Longing to wrap Ricky up in my arms, hold his head to my chest and close my eyes flooded me to the point my eyes stung.

I dropped the topic of Ricky, knowing my dad wouldn't bend, but that didn't stop my mind from focusing on him with every beat of my heart.

Hopefully, Ricky would prove a slave to the attraction between us, and I'd see him sooner than later. I just hoped he didn't take off for back east before I got a chance to entice him to take a step in my direction instead.

7

RICKY

I hooked up with a contractor on Monday morning and a shaking of hands confirmed our agreement the old fashioned way. His electrician had busted up his SUV and his right arm in a bad accident two weeks earlier, and a new home build sat half-finished.

It probably helped that we'd both shown up for our meeting on Harleys. While Craig wasn't a Viper, he knew of the club. He also knew Klingon, and a friend of Klingon was a friend of his.

Job landed.

I worked ten-hour days the next four in a row, the scent of sawdust and freshly cut lumber easing my antsy feet. Nothing like a construction site... The chance to help build a home, provide for a family, gave me a sense of satisfaction it did for most contractors I'd worked with over the years. While not caring for my own family, it still gave me that good feeling inside.

Something I hadn't felt in too long.

I slept a bit better at night, and woke up every morning with the sun, ready for that same sense of accomplishment.

Friday night I rode my bike to the Viper's club at Klingon's insistence, parking alongside a custom, neon green chopper with "Pennies" written in script across the tank.

I met the copper-haired jokester inside along with the other officers at a round table. Butcher greeted me with zero warmth, but at least he didn't stare at me with the promise of death. The officers shared beer and bullshit while I sat dry as fuck, hands resting on my thighs, checking the place out.

The interior was stucco like the exterior, a tan color similar to the desert, but pictures and paintings hung all over the place. Biker families. Groups of brothers from road trips—Rushmore, Devil's Tower, and more than a dozen of Sturgis events.

Balls cracked from the pool tables at the back of the club, and a couple brothers tossed darts like Hammer and Crow loved doing back home. I'd worked with the two brothers' construction company for a couple years before leaving New England, and even though I missed their comradery, I didn't find myself wishing to head back.

A long bar spread along the wall to my left, manned by two pledges. I counted six club whores working the room, but not a single one got a rise out of me. It seemed my dick decided Casey was it—and *that* was it.

"Room's available out back." Klingon's declaration aimed my way pulled me back to the round table. "Figured if you're going to stick around for a while, it'd be better here than a hotel."

He peered at me, but I glanced at his officers before replying. Prophet nodded. Pennies seemed to be grinning, not that I could see his mouth through his whiskers. Crank lifted his beer in silent agreement, and Butcher eyed his president rather than me, his face blank as fuck.

No question what he thought of Klingon's suggestion, though.

"Appreciate the offer," I said, turning my focus back on Klingon who'd obviously tossed out that idea without consulting his Sergeant at Arms, "but I'm good."

"Move in," Butcher ordered, turning to face me, the hard glint returning to his eyes.

I'd kept my mouth shut at the BBQ, but I'd since decided I wouldn't back down. He held no position of authority over me. "So you can keep an eye on me?" I asked, leaning to put my elbows on the table—and holding his gaze, needing him to know I had a backbone even if I did respect his position.

"Fucking right." Butcher nodded, staring me down. "It's my job to protect this club, and until I know what you're about, I want you close."

"I'm not *about* anything. I'm not the enemy," I said, my voice hard as pissiness over his assumption roused inside me. God knows I'd been judged enough in my thirty-nine years. Didn't need some fucker who barely knew me putting labels on me.

"Not yet, you aren't."

Klingon backhanded Butcher's shoulder, the crazy fuck. Butcher glared at him while I fought to keep from wanting to smash in Casey's father's nose. "Leave him alone, Butcher. Ryker vouches for him, so he's good in my book."

Butcher didn't reply, but his glare said enough. He might trust Klingon, but he sure as fuck didn't trust me. I had to respect his loyalty to his colors and his title, but wondered if he feared his daughter's rebellious nature more than he did me.

"My daughter is off limits."

Fucking line drawn in the sand. *Fuck.* I didn't twitch although my scowl wanted to permanently indent my forehead. "I got that hint loud and clear."

"You make a move before I have you figured out —fucking categorized where you belong—I'll end you without regret."

Casey would sure as fuck have a thing or two to say to him if he made good on that promise, but I kept my mouth shut. Best not to dig my own goddamn grave. Besides, telling the truth would confirm his worst nightmares—I was a fucking addict loser who hadn't been able to protect the woman I'd loved.

The worst kind of man. Hardly worthy of a woman like Casey.

I didn't look away, though, and our stare down lasted long enough Pennies called for another round.

Klingon knocked his knuckles on the table to get our attention. "Enough."

Butcher looked away first, obeying his president.

Klingon turned the conversation to the young punks from LA trying to encroach on their territory.

Again, club business, stuff I shouldn't have been privy to. I only half listened as my thoughts strayed back to Butcher's daughter. Casey had become the new haunter of my dreams, and even though I emptied my balls countless times to the memory of the way she moved on stage, I continued to tell myself she wasn't my type and pursuing her would only land me in a sand-filled grave beneath the baking sun.

More fucking guilt over my body wanting to move on from Annie fueled the rest of those goddamn demons, but at least I wasn't salivating for a bottle of whiskey in response. That part of my past, at least, seemed to have quieted.

The decision to stay in Vegas seemed right to me. Between the job I'd landed and the Vipers—besides Butcher—filling that loneliness for friends I hadn't realized lay in my soul, I was pretty sure I'd found my new home.

"The fuck they doing here?" Prophet asked.

I shot my attention to the club's door at his question but no one entered. Realizing I'd zoned out from their conversation, I turned my focus back on Prophet.

His arms crossed, legs spread wide like he was ready to throw down or squeeze off a few dozen shots himself to end them all. I realized he spoke about the punks from L.A.

"That little shit didn't give us anything last weekend," Pennies muttered, his beard barely rustling with the words.

Klingon nodded, and I realized they spoke of the guy he'd snagged from the motel. "Leftie called me a few hours ago," he said. "Told me they set up an exchange for firearms with him. Warned me they mean business."

"We confirm that safe house over on Estes Avenue?" Butcher asked, his blue eyes hard as steel, a sweating bottle of beer held between his two paws.

Klingon glanced at Prophet who nodded. "Can't have little shits coming in here thinking they can take over."

"Gonna make an example of them?" Balboa asked, cracking his knuckles like he was jonesing for a fight.

"Fucking right." Klingon eyed his men—me included—one by one, his voice lowering and shoulders hunching as he leaned toward the table's center. "We need to do away with their whole goddamn crew. Leftie told me he set up an exchange with them and invited us to the party. Once the exchange happens, he and his men have our backs. He keeps the cash, we keep the guns."

A few more details and questions tossed back and forth, and I figured out Leftie must be the Vipers' firearms supplier in the black market I knew the Vegas boys dealt in. Why the fuck a young gang thought they could make a deal with Leftie behind the Vipers' backs and live to tell about it beat the shit out of me.

"They're only eight strong, last Leftie had heard," Klingon said. "Should be an easy take down."

"When?" Butcher asked, his gaze set on Klingon's face.

"One week from Sunday. Midnight," Klingon answered and emptied his beer. "I'm going to meet up with Leftie and we'll talk it out. We'll get plans set in stone at next week's club meeting."

The men around the table agreed, their respect and trust in their president evident in relaxed postures and confident gazes. Vigil held similar respect in the club back home. But respecting him came easy. He's always put the club first, his brothers' welfare above his own.

I rubbed at my chest as the conversation turned to other shit not related to club business, and I decided to call it a night, realizing it was time to call my brother.

Butcher's hard gaze followed me clear out the door.

Remembering it was only around dinner time back east, I waited another hour in my room, flicking through the cable channels without finding shit to watch.

Bored and giving into loneliness since I'd opened myself up to people again, I put through my call earlier than planned. Vigil picked up after the first ring as though he'd had his cell in hand, waiting for me to reach out.

"Ricky." His voice sounded pleased to hear from me, not a hint of fear or anger.

"Hey."

"How's Vegas?"

Biding his time before lighting into me, or was he truly interested? I tended toward the first, knowing my brother. "Good. Been over to the club, but I'm sure you heard."

"Yeah. Klingon said you're looking good—doing good. Fucking glad to hear it."

A rush of warmth for my older brother filled me, actually stinging my fucking eyes. "I needed space, but I'm sorry I left the way I did."

"Your colors are here whenever you're ready to come back."

"I'm not coming back." The words left me with a finality I hadn't expected to spew out, but I felt the decision deep inside my bones at voicing them.

Vigil wasn't quick to respond, but I held my tongue as he probably struggled not to order me to get my ass home. "Guess a fresh start was what you needed," he finally said, and the disappointment in his tone hurt my fucking chest. "Klingon said something about you transferring to his club, but I was hoping for a different outcome."

"I need a new beginning," I said and swallowed against the thickness in my throat. "Not saying I won't visit sometimes, but Mass isn't my home anymore."

"Demons chased you out," Vigil said, his tone hinting at anger, a grumble at the very least.

"I'm thinking it's for the best."

"Those fuckers still clawing at your head?"

I closed my eyes and leaned back against the headboard, the quiet drone of my room's TV the only sound. "Not nearly as much."

"Booze?"

"No desire for it."

"Drugs?"

"Not at all." That was one hard limit I'd drawn after losing Annie—and stuck with. Gave me hope to kick the booze for good, too.

"Thank fuck."

"So, tell me what the fuck is going on," I said, ready to catch up rather than focus on my shit. "Klingon said something about Michelle's real name being Mila?"

Vigil filled me in on the previous couple of weeks since I'd taken off. Turned out the woman he'd been salivating over wasn't who he'd thought. She and her son had been in the Witness Protection Program for helping to put the Demons, our old rivals, behind bars.

Knowing my brother and his voice like I did, I could tell that trouble had come knocking but I couldn't outright ask over the line. "You have to clean up any shit lately?"

"A little. Nothing we couldn't handle, though." Vigil's said, his voice nonchalant as fuck. "That stench won't be bothering us ever again."

"Sorry I wasn't there to help you out."

"Our brothers had my back. You weren't in the right head space for scraping dog shit off the bottom of your boots."

Vigil spoke truth, but it still stung that I hadn't been there for him like he'd always been for me.

"Shallow?" I asked in code about graves that might have been dug after cleaning up that shit and thinking about the one we'd dug together deep in the woods of Maine.

"Fishies."

I nodded to myself, knowing the Vipers' cleaners tended toward erasing all trace of evidence we'd snuffed out a life or ten. "Did you claim her?"

"And her son," he didn't hesitate to respond.

I snorted a laugh. "Thought you were sworn off kids."

"Devon's a teenager—more my friend than Mila's baggage."

"Well, shit." I still smiled, imagining my brother being a dad of sorts. He'd definitely be the better of us two since I tended toward the darker side like our father had.

My smile faded quick as fuck even if that demon had been buried decades ago. It was the guilt over not protecting our mother that stung like swarming hornets. Add in Annie's death, and I cursed my protective nature that always failed loved ones.

But Vigil's never failed.

Fucking bitterness slithered through the other

demons, trying to raise his ugly head, but I grit my teeth against it. Yes, my brother was a better man than me, didn't have that darkness of our bastard father who'd caved to his own addictions time and time again. I swallowed that bitter pill as I'd done dozens of times in the past even though I couldn't rid my mind of it.

"Sorry for the words before I left," I forced myself to say, hating that apologies seemed to be all I was capable of.

"Don't worry about it." Vigil brushed it off like he always did when I apologized for spewing shit.

I decided to let it go, allowed him to make things okay until the next time I lost my shit.

"So you transferring or what? I'll put the paper-work through if that's what you really want."

"I disrespected my colors, Vigil."

"You disrespected yourself, brother. Letting those demons get the best of you. You needed space to breathe. I get that. Your brothers here at home get that. Not a single one holds it over your head or demanded an ass-kicking for you leaving your cut and colors behind."

And why the fuck I felt the need to live a life away from that kind of friendship beat the hell outta me.

"Haven't decided on transferring," I stated a half-truth. If not for Casey and her father being the Sergeant at Arms issue, I probably would have agreed to joining Klingon's club without hesitation. I wanted it. Figured I'd do it eventually—if I could get past wanting to bone and hold Casey in my arms for fucking forever.

"Well, I'm putting it through." Vigil's statement held a tone that suggested I didn't argue—so I didn't.

We hung up a few minutes later, and I felt lonelier than I had before calling him. Staring at the water-stained ceiling of my hotel room, I considered it being a weekend. Friday night. One week since I'd seen Casey dancing.

I'd kept my distance, obeyed her father's wishes, but it wasn't a crime for a man to go to a strip joint and enjoy the sights. Just a guy sitting alone in a dark corner, hard as fuck for a tiny dancer...

Less than three hours earlier Butcher had warned me to stay away from her. How far was away? Two feet? Ten? Stay out of her personal space? He told me to not make a move on her, and watching certainly wasn't the same as hitting on.

Loop-hole decided upon, ten minutes later, I pushed open the strip joint's door and found a place to hide so I could fuel my fantasies.

8

CASEY

"He's here." Skin Tight's declaration pulled my focus off my mirror.

Heart leaping, I capped my lip gloss and tossed it onto the cluttered makeup atop my "work desk" as us dancers called the only bit of personal space allotted us in the club. "Ricky?" I asked, keeping my voice low while eyeing the other two girls getting ready for their sets.

He nodded, and I hopped up. "How much time have I got?"

"Maybe fifteen."

I moved past him, knowing I really had less since I hadn't dressed for my turn on stage.

"Casey..."

Turning, I clasped the changing room's door handle, my entire body buzzing to move.

"Don't get me in trouble." Skin Tight's lips flatlined.

I winked. "Wouldn't dream of it." And I wouldn't. I messed up a lot in my life, but prided myself in owning up to those mistakes. Ricky wouldn't be one. I felt it in my bones, in my heart. Just had to be careful in the steps I took.

A few steady breaths did nothing to settle my racing heart as I hurried down the hallway toward the lounge. I slipped into the cavernous room—between sets, so no lights flashed or music slammed overhead.

My focus went straight to the corner Ricky had hid in before, but he wasn't there. Huffing, I glanced around, and that delicious shiver slid over me a second before I found him in the opposite corner, closer to the stage.

An overhead light close by lit up one side of his face, and even if I hadn't been able to make out his eyes across the distance, knowing we'd connected said enough. Grinning, I moved toward him, a woman on a mission.

He glanced at the exit, his shoulders tensing, but I cut into his line of sight, forcing his attention back on me. I stood between him and escape, and I wasn't about to let him take off like he'd done the Saturday before without talking to me.

"Hey." I slipped into the chair beside his—closest to the door.

"Hey." A muscle in his jaw twitched, but he held my stare, his eyes full of conflicting emotions I could only guess at.

The desire to heal the pain I could easily see, though, sent an ache through me. "Whatcha drinking?" I decided to keep it light, my gaze flitting to the soda in front of him.

"Coke."

"And rum?"

"Nope."

I raised an eyebrow, but remembered he'd only had lemonade at the party the weekend before. "Not a drinker, huh?"

He finally glanced away from me. "I'm an alcoholic."

I appreciated the honesty, the vulnerability he showed by admitting as such. "Hanging out with the Vipers and not drinking can't be easy. I'm proud of you."

Ricky's focus jerked back to my face, and I smiled, that damn desire inside me to heal or soothe him doubling in intensity. "Thanks," he murmured, studying my eyes, my face, as though tucking the sight of me into the deepest parts of his memory in the event I decided to judge him for his honesty—or because he planned to leave town.

"Going away soon?" I asked, a pang in my heart lessening my smile.

"No plans to, no."

Relief flooded through me, and I relaxed with a rushed exhale. "Glad to hear that, Ricky."

"This can't happen," he muttered, leaning forward onto the table, still holding my gaze.

"What's that?"

"This." He motioned between us. "You're Butcher's kid."

"I'm not a kid."

"No." Ricky glanced at my chest and back up real quick. "You're not a kid, but you're off limits, all the same."

"And if I wasn't?" I scooted closer, propping my elbow on the table, chin in hand, letting him see exactly what I wanted in my eyes.

"Pushy little brat."

"I like to call it *determined*," I countered with a grin, but it didn't lessen his scowl. "Goes along with that independent spirit of mine."

Thumping bass sounded as we stared one another down, matching the heightened ones in my chest. With the music, I wouldn't be able to hear him even if he answered.

Ricky licked his lower lip as the strobe lights went off announcing a dancer, but he kept his focus on my face. His gaze hardened as though he'd come to a conclusion, and he crooked a finger.

I leaned even closer, my eyelids fluttering shut. *Yes, please...*

He grasped my chin and turned my face toward stage, his hot breath against my ear rather than my lips.

"If you weren't off limits," he murmured into my ear, "I'd bend you over like she's doing."

My eyelids popped back open, my breath catching.

Sylvia bent clear over, grasping her ankles, her thong strung tight between her ass cheeks, and the boys directly behind her hooted their approval.

Ricky's lips coasted over the shell of my ear, sending a shiver over my skin, pebbling every inch. "I'd grasp those lush ass cheeks of yours and eat the hell out of your pussy. Wouldn't stop licking or fucking you with my tongue until you came all over my face, screaming my name."

Holy shit balls.

I gulped, a rush of wetness leaking from me. "And then?" I asked even though he wouldn't hear me over the rock song Sylvia stripped to.

"Then I'd give you what you want," he continued as though he'd heard me. "Every inch of my dick so far up your tight pussy you'd lose your breath."

"Oh God." My pussy spasmed with need, and I shuddered.

"But you *are* off limits, tiny dancer." Ricky bit my lobe, and I groaned, my eyelids slamming shut once more. "Doesn't mean I can't watch you on stage, though, right?"

I nodded, unable to voice a goddamn word, Ricky had me so strung tight.

"Will you dance for me, Casey? Give me something to remember while I'm fucking my fist later tonight since I can't have you under me?" He sat back, his grip still on my jaw, turning me toward him.

His eyes blazed with blue flame enough to scorch me from the inside out, and in that moment, I would have given him whatever the hell he wanted, Skin Tight and Daddy be damned. Lap dance? Hell, yeah. Blow job with everyone watching? If it's what he wanted, I wouldn't hesitate. Bend me over the small table in front of us, claiming my body as his own?

A shudder rippled over me.

"I'll give you whatever you want, Ricky Capone," I stated loudly so he'd hear even though inches separated our face.

His gaze dropped to my lips. "Dance for me."

I left him alone at the table, my panties a soaked mess beneath my skin-tight jeans, trembling throughout my body making it hard to turn the handle of the door leading back to the employees only area. I nearly poked out an eye while swiping on another layer of mascara. I couldn't clasp the front snap of the corset I'd decided on for my first set.

My heart pounded in my chest as I waited backstage for my song to start. I'd never been so nervous in my life. Dancing usually came easy—without thought, but the tension riding me when I needed that pole to be Ricky...

The whine of a guitar announced my song, and I sauntered on stage, my focus going straight to my man in the corner closest to the stage. He sat back, a small smirk on his face, but I wanted lust. I narrowed my gaze and set to work, making him sweat in his chair, shifting to relieve the ache that must have intensified with every shift, every gyration of my body.

I leaned against the pole, holding his gaze while arching my back and grasping the cool metal overhead. Breasts jutting out and nearly spilling from the corset, I ground my ass against the pole imagining it was him behind me, eating me out like he'd said he wanted to do.

Lips parted to suck oxygen into my starved lungs, I held his gaze, lost in the dance of need between us.

I didn't bother with the other patrons. Didn't spare a single man cat calling at me one second of my time. Ricky held my attention as no man ever had—or ever would again, I had no doubt.

While I never believed in love at first sight, I couldn't argue the pull between us, the knowing of something that couldn't be denied. Lust? Absolutely, but so much more. What it was exactly, I didn't know, but I sure as hell would find out.

Daddy wouldn't stop me.

Ricky's demons wouldn't stop me.

If either man thought they were more stubborn than me, if either man thought they knew what was best for me, they had another think coming.

9

———

RICKY

She kept her eyes on me through the entire song, making my dick so damn hard I could have pounded nails with the fucking thing. The whole grinding of her ass against that pole? Goddamn, her sass killed me. It was one of those *I know she knows what I'm thinking* moments, and we both lived it, the proof in her nipples strained against black leather and the wetness smeared between her thighs when she'd bent clear over like the earlier dancer, letting me see exactly what imagining me eating her out did to her body.

Forward, rebellious vixen.

If her daddy ever found out...

The second she slipped behind stage, I hurried outside, avoiding the manager when he flagged me down like he wanted a few hundred bills for another private moment with Casey. Obviously, the man didn't know David "Butcher" Dawes as well as I did —and I barely knew the fucker.

I sat in my truck, hard as hell, hands on the steering wheel, able to watch both the front and side employee entrance from my spot at the far edge of the lot. An hour of torture passed while I waited for Casey to leave—I wasn't about to let her head home alone, unprotected. Knowing she hadn't snuck out under my watch, I guessed she had a second set.

I stayed put, knowing having to watch her again would make my self-control cave to lust. Sitting with her for those brief moments had been one of the best moments of my life besides tasting her mouth the weekend before. Touching the soft skin of her chin a gift from heaven I didn't deserve. Breathing in the scent of her sweet peaches skin...

Having her words of edification? Her being proud of me?

Fuck.

I rubbed my chest, my brow furrowed, knowing every off-limit touch had been so damn worth it. No one had said that kind of thing to me since Auntie Jeanie, and I found myself wanting to stay sober for far more than just myself. I soaked that shit in—

wanted her to be proud of me for the rest of my goddamn life.

A black Excursion pulled up in front of the employee door, and two seconds later, Casey stepped outside and hopped in. Scowling, I eyed the driver, paying attention like I hadn't when he'd pulled in, taking note of his blond, curly hair—Balboa, Klingon's enforcer.

Jealousy, more like hot rage, lit to life in my gut. Was she fucking him behind her father's back? I hadn't noticed anyone but Butcher act all cave-man over her ass...

What the fuck?

I turned the key and pulled out after the SUV, following at a distance, my mind a cluster fuck of rage, lust, and jealousy.

They stayed on back roads, and twice I almost lost them in my need to stay back far enough Balboa wouldn't know he had a tail. It shouldn't have been easy. He should have noted my truck after the third turn. Was he so caught up in Casey beside him that he lost focus? Did she suck down his cock, distracting him from being ever watchful over his brother's daughter?

Teeth grinding, I held steady, slowing and putting my truck into park as Balboa pulled into a driveway deep in a residential neighborhood we'd entered.

Casey hopped out of his vehicle with a bounce in her step, the flood lights springing to life and show-casing her outline in the tight as fuck jeans I'd wanted to strip off her earlier that night.

She waved at Balboa, smiling brightly.

He took a different route out of the neighbor-hood, and I sat unmoving, my stomach a twist of fucking knots until the lights in her house went out a half-hour later.

"Tomorrow, I'll find out if they're fucking," I vowed to myself and grimaced as the truth of Casey Dawes' effect on me cleared fully inside my brain—fucking addiction. I'd traded one for another, it seemed, and that thought did not sit well in my gut or head.

My demons, though, they had a fucking riot and it was well into the night before they quit trying to drag me under and let me sleep.

———

Klingon invited me to church the next day, and I sat against the wall of his office rather than at the table he insisted upon, my arms crossed, my eyes on

Balboa even as my stomach twisted over the thought of addiction and jealousy. He seemed completely at ease beside Butcher, shooting the shit and laughing like he hadn't a care in the world as they all sat around a huge ass table in the office's center. I imagined if he'd been fucking Casey or having her suck his dick in secret, he'd be a little more uncomfortable around her father.

I know for me, a mere blow job wouldn't be the end to the night if I was fucking her. Hell, no. I'd have sniffed after her ass straight through her front door and taken her the second it shut behind us.

"Next Sunday, we'll meet here at nine," Klingon said, and I shot my focus toward him at the head of the table. "We're going to pull in a handful of brothers to go with us." He nodded at me. "Ricky's going."

I didn't argue even though he hadn't asked if I wanted to accompany them. How he knew I would have their back regardless of my short time with them, and the fact I didn't wear colors? I had no fucking clue. My nod of agreement sent his attention back to his officers.

We still hadn't discussed my transfer—and I still wasn't ready to make a final decision, but I would have their backs. Always.

I felt Butcher's stare, but let it slide. Maybe my going along and offering his brothers support would prove my loyalty. While the idea it might soften him toward my wanting his daughter rose as well, I reminded myself I didn't want her. Her light fucking blinded me to the point of mindlessness, something I couldn't stomach happening to me ever again.

I still found myself in the club's corner that night, a weak man to my need. *Just to watch*, I told myself. Not to touch, not to taste, not to even steal a moment of her time to soak in her voice, her warmth.

She slipped onto the chair beside me in another pair of tight as fuck jeans and a tank top dipped low enough to make my mouth water for a mouthful of her tits. "You're back," she said, breathless as fuck and smelling sweet as a ripe peach.

"Can't stay the fuck away," I grunted, hating my weakness and knowing we were on a crash course headed for disaster if her father ever found out. At least he hadn't confronted me and I would have been faced with lying to cover my ass.

Fucking weak. Dishonest. Disloyal bastard...

Her saucy smirk jerked my dick in my jeans even as my demons howled. "Can't say I'm sorry to hear that."

"I'll bet not." Keeping my focus on her face, I drank down some tonic until it burned my throat, but the ice cold drink didn't cool me down one fucking bit.

"So, does this mean you're going to give me what I want?" she said with a wider smirk, leaning forward enough I could fill my eyes with her cleavage.

I allowed myself the pleasure of receiving that damn gift, thoughts of sliding my lubed up dick through that soft flesh pulling a groan from me.

"See something you like?"

Fuck, the husk in her voice... *So goddamn weak.* "You know I do."

"So give me five minutes after my set."

"No."

"Just one more taste of your mouth, Ricky. That's all I'm asking for."

I imagined she wanted a hell of a lot more than that, but I rode a fine line with Casey, and the soul I'd realized I still owned upon arriving in Nevada would be fucked if I gave in.

"No," I forced out through gritted teeth, inwardly telling my demons to fuck off.

"I could change your mind," she said with a twinkle in her eye, the damn little vixen.

"You could try," I said without meaning to tempt her to prove her determination.

"I'll take that bet." She held out her hand, a confident grin fixed on her smiling lips.

Fuck, but I couldn't help myself. I took her hand.

"I change your mind, and I get what I want," she murmured with heat in her eyes that oozed pre-cum from my dick.

"And what if I win?"

"You won't." She winked and left me sitting there hard as nails and cursing my inability to stay the fuck away from her.

Twenty minutes later, she danced on stage, making my mouth drier than the entire goddamn desert surrounding Vegas. I was a parched man stumbling through what I thought had been life, and Casey offered what I craved.

Her eyes begged before she exited the stage.

I shook my head, cursing myself a fool. Again, I headed out to my truck, determined to see her home safely even if that's all Balboa once more showed up to do.

10

CASEY

The fucking balls on Ricky—stubborn as hell, more self-control than any man I'd ever met.

He left again before I got a chance to sneak back into the lounge after my set to talk to him. Same as the night before, I danced my second set with only the eyes of salivating pigs glued to me when all I'd wanted were the intense blue of one Mr. Capone.

At least he'd openly admitted to wanting me, and given the opportunity, I expected I could get him to cave. I also expected he feared that fact, thus the taking off before I could talk to him again.

I needed to find out what the fuck his story was so I could break down his damn walls, get what I wanted—both physically and to help heal the pain in his eyes over whoever she was, that *her* he'd spoken of right before we'd kissed.

An hour later, I sat in Balboa's SUV, ignoring the country music he had turned up same as every night he drove me home. Daddy's watchdog, Balboa had been seeing me home ever since I started dancing at ST's six months earlier after UNLV had shut down my dreams of becoming a pediatrician.

Not once did he complain about my ruining his weekends. Not once did he gripe about staying out late and not getting anything in return. He'd never hit on me. Didn't even give me the side eye.

"Are you gay?" I asked, rolling my head along the headrest to look at him.

"What?" he half snorted and choked on a cough.

"Are. You. Gay?"

A muscle ticked in his jaw.

"'Cuz it's totally cool if you are. I won't tell anyone."

"Why you gotta ask personal shit like that, Casey?" he grumbled, his brow furrowed as he pulled into my neighborhood. "Always pushing and probing, you nosey little shit."

Headlights flashed behind us, and I took note of the truck a hundred yards or so behind us, being ever vigilant as Daddy had taught me. That same truck had followed us home the night before, and Balboa hadn't noticed.

I'd recognized the truck, and since Ricky hadn't come knocking but left after I'd shut off the lights the night before, I knew he was seeing to my safety.

God, Daddy would be impressed if only he'd give my man a shot to prove himself.

"Just wondered," I said, still eyeing the truck. "I've never seen you bring a woman to the club, and you don't seem interested in any of the whores whenever they're around."

"I'm not gay," he bit the words out while making another right-hand turn. "But you haven't been around much lately to know that fact."

I thought about pushing the topic, but the truck behind us turned, too—and the street light shone down on the vehicle.

Definitely Ricky.

My heart took to the races, catching my damn breath even as my heart warmed at his personally wanting to see me home safely.

"Okay," I murmured to Balboa, letting the matter of his sexuality rest even though it was none of my damn business, anyway. I just thought we'd become friends of a sort over the previous six months of his being my chauffeur and babysitter.

Balboa stopped in front of my little bungalow, and I watched in my periphery as Ricky parked two blocks away.

"See you next weekend," I said, hopping from the SUV.

He nodded, the vehicle's interior light showcasing a deep blush over his cheeks.

"Promise I won't tell," I whispered and winked, slamming the passenger door before he could deny what I'd guessed.

He had to know my father and Klingon wouldn't care. I didn't know the other officers enough to know what sort of flak he might catch, but my heart went out to him. Being a Vicious Viper and gay probably wouldn't mix.

I headed inside, tingles racing over my skin, but kept the interior lights out so I could peek out my front window to see if Ricky stayed put after Balboa drove off.

He stayed, and I imagined he gripped his steering wheel, knuckles white as he fought the need to come to me. Unable to even think about his driving off again, I opened the door the second Balboa's SUV turned out of sight.

I leaned against my door jam, focused on Ricky's truck even though I couldn't see his face inside the dark interior. Dancing hadn't been enticement enough, so what could I possibly do but hope he'd drive closer, pull into my driveway, and climb out of his sexy as fuck truck, willing to give into what brewed between us?

"Come on, babe," I whispered, barely moving my lips. "Get your ass over here and let's disobey my daddy."

He held strong, the slight hum of the truck's engine reaching me in the stillness of midnight.

Patience wasn't something I was known for—I crooked my finger and pointed at my feet.

The waiting fucking *killed*.

11

RICKY

No harm in watching her dance, I'd told myself.

No harm in sneaking into her house since there was no one around to witness my weakness, either. What Butcher didn't know wouldn't hurt him. How many times had I used that excuse in my past to hide my sins?

Fuck.

I gripped the damn steering wheel hard as fuck, and when she crooked her finger at me, pointing to her feet, I groaned. She wanted me to worship at her goddamn feet, and I realized I would offer up what was left of my goddamn soul to please her.

Fucking weak prick.

That demon didn't stop me from slamming the

truck into gear and approaching her house in near silence.

She held her stance against the doorjamb, acting all sexy at ease while I hopped out of my truck and moved toward her, but her parted lips and straining nipples through her tank betrayed what she wanted.

Tension strung tight between us, and the second I could make out the black of her pupils eating away at the sky blue color surrounding them, I knew I was a goner. Without even touching her, I knew Casey Dawes would own me, every miserable bit of what heart I had left in my chest, every thought, every minute of the rest of my life would be hers.

She was my addiction, and being the independent woman she was, Casey would leave when she'd gotten her fill. She certainly didn't need me—just wanted me.

Even knowing she would be the death of me, I couldn't fucking say no.

Weak. You'll let her down ... you'll fail her...

I told the fuckers to shut up and focused on stealing what moments I could. Energy like a live wire radiated between us as I stepped up onto the stoop, and she backed into the house, my stalking footsteps taking me forward. The second I passed over the threshold, I kicked the door shut behind me.

Our breaths sounded loud in the silence of her home, and I pressed my palm against her chest, the thump of her heart, the catch of her breath like life to me. I pushed, and she backed against the wall, her hands braced beside her thighs.

She licked her lower lip, her gaze dropping to my mouth. "Kiss me."

A slow smirk lifted my lips. She might think she'd gotten me to cave to our mutual want and won our little bet, but she wasn't about to control me when it came to our fucking.

I sank to my knees, my hands on her hips. "You didn't say where," I murmured, leaning in to press my lips against the crotch of her jeans.

Fuck, I could smell the tang of her arousal through the denim, and I needed a taste.

Right the fuck now.

I made quick work of her jean's button and zipper, yanking them to her knees.

Her hands on my head, she kicked off her shoes and helped me rid her of her jeans. White, virginal cotton...

I slid my thumb down over her, groaning at the wetness seeping through the material between her thighs. "Fucking soaked," I groaned the words, my mouth watering.

"Only for you," she rasped as I hooked my thumb beneath her panties and pulled them to the side.

Glistening sweetness...

Fuck, my balls ached.

I slid her panties off rather than shove my face into her pussy. I'd created an image in both our minds when I'd whispered in her ear, and I planned to deliver.

"Turn around," I said, slipping the soaked cotton off her feet.

She did as told, and I shifted her hips back, giving her space to bend over.

"Grab your ankles, baby, and hold on tight." I grasped her ass cheeks and dove in before she fully bent, licking up her slit, my dick leaking at the tang of her cream coating my tongue. I'd always enjoyed eating the hell out of a pussy, but Casey tasted sweet as could be, a fucking drug if ever I'd imbibed—and I had. Too much.

Addicted? Worse than the first shot of heroine to a virgin vein. But in that moment, I didn't give a fuck.

She moaned something about God with a few curses mixed in, but all I could focus on was the taste of her, the satiny feel of her labia between my lips, the hard nub of her pearl-like clit.

I rimmed her pussy with the tip of my tongue, denying her when she begged for more. I licked her asshole, pressing in enough she relaxed, tightening my balls to the point of pain. Without a doubt, I knew she'd give me that too if I asked.

Sitting back on my haunches pulled a whimper from her, but I gave her two fingers instead, burying them inside her creamy pussy, teeth clenched against the tightness. Her blonde hair hung to the floor, her eyes closed and lips parted as I slowly fucked her with my fingers, twisting them to rub along her G-spot.

"Ricky," she whispered, her legs shaking.

"Hmm?" I slid my other thumb over her perfect little rosebud of a hole. The skin puckered beneath my touch and relaxed again as I applied light pressure, the saliva I'd left behind lube enough to not hurt her even if she'd never had a dick or finger up her ass.

"Fuck," she groaned when I slid past the ring of muscle with little resistance, and I settled in to finger fuck a climax out of her. "Oh, fuck." She licked her lips and panted as I slowly worked her pussy, my thumb pressing in deeper with each retreat of my fingers.

"Don't stop," she whimpered when I slid my fingers out of her pussy to rub over her bare pubis.

I gave her needy little pussy my other thumb, working both in opposition, leaving my slickened fingers free to play with her clit.

"Oh God, oh God, oh God—" Her voice cut off with a shriek, her pussy clamping down on my thumb, creamy cum oozing into my palm.

Talk about fucking satisfaction. I'd never enjoyed hearing a woman come like Casey did, her gasps and whimpers while coming down beyond the high of any cocaine. I sucked my fingers clean but needed more. So much fucking more.

"I want you," she whispered as I licked her cum off her pussy, groaning at the taste of her. "Please, Ricky."

Casey *had* become my drug of choice—and I was fucked.

12

CASEY

Ricky moved away, and I lifted and turned, sagging my back against the wall since my knees were weak as hell from the most explosive climax I'd ever experienced. He stood, fists clenched and chest heaving, peering at me from heavy-lidded eyes.

His cock strained inside his jeans, but he held still.

"Ricky?" I whispered, afraid he would bolt on me again.

The second he gave in completely to what we both wanted, his shoulders lowered and guilt flooded his eyes. "Your father is going to gut me wide open."

"He doesn't need to know," I reasoned with the first thing to pop into my head, cursing myself immediately after thinking Ricky might take it as my wanting to hide him like he wasn't good enough—

"Bedroom." He rasped the word as though incapable of saying anything else.

I didn't bother with a sassy smirk but stepped past him, knowing he would follow my swaying, bare ass back the short hallway. Needing to see him, I turned the dimmers on enough to be able to watch him fuck me, but not so bright to make us squint in the sudden light.

He grasped my hips again before I could turn, burying his face in my neck, the hard length of his entire body pressing against my back.

"Sorry," he whispered, and I turned, grasping his face in my hands.

"Don't you dare fucking apologize to me or anyone else—unless you're married?" That last though seized my heart right the fuck up.

"I'm not married."

"Girlfriend?"

"No."

"Boyfriend back in Boston?"

"No."

A smile accompanied the restart of my heart. "Then don't you dare apologize for wanting me."

He laid claim to my mouth before I could inhale, his hands ripping at my tank, stinging my skin, but I couldn't find two fucks to give. His aggression made me hot as hell.

I shoved my hands beneath his shirt, my fingers finding abs to die for, my touch pulling a slow hiss from his mouth. Low-slung jeans hung on hips indented with that muscle women lusted over. Fuck, he was cut like a god.

Ricky grasped my hair in his hands, devouring my mouth, obliterating all thought but the taste of his sweet breath, the soft cushion of his lips, and the nip of his teeth.

My fingers fumbled with the button and zipper keeping me from touching him.

"Fuck." He jerked back, ripping his shirt off overhead and shoving his jeans down before I realized he wasn't tearing away to leave me. He hopped from one foot to the other while yanking off his boots, but I was too far gone with lust to laugh at his antics.

Ricky finally stilled, standing naked and vulnerable in front of me, head lowered and gaze on my face.

Holy fucking Christ... I drank him in, eyeing the

tattoo scrolled over his shoulder and chest, his pecs like chiseled stone, the abs I'd explored with my fingertips deeply grooved. His cock jerked beneath my stare, the tip oozing with pre-cum.

My pussy spasmed, and I forced my attention southward, loving the bulge of his muscular thighs and prominent calf muscles. Nothing better than a man who knew how to take care of his God-gifted body.

I unclasped my bra, dropping it to the floor, and stood trembling while he took his turn drinking me in, gaze roaming down over me. He grasped the base of his dick and squeezed, slowly working his length a few seconds while studying the apex of my thighs. Lust darkened the blue of his eyes to midnight, and until he focused on my face again, my body hovered on the edge of another climax.

"If I'm going to get gutted for this, I want it all," Ricky said, his voice husky and sexy as hell, like a man teetering on the edge of reason. Fuck, if his tone and slow jack of his dick without embarrassment didn't leak wetness from my pussy. "Birth control?"

"Yes," I whispered.

The muscle in his jaw ticked. "Clean?"

I nodded. "You?"

He dipped his head once.

"I'm going to fuck you bare, Casey. Don't want anything but you wrapped around my dick."

"Yes."

Ricky took a step closer, studying my face while rubbing his thumb over the pre-cum beaded at the top of his dick.

My mouth watered, and I swallowed.

"You don't know me," he murmured, smearing the pre-cum down his length rather than feed it to me like I wanted. "How can you trust me?"

"I just do." I lifted my focus to his face as he stopped inches away from me. "I can feel this—here." I placed my hand on his chest. "This is right. *You're* right."

He kissed me. God, how he kissed me—like I was his final breath, the final heartbeat left to his life, and I gave him everything in return, the heat, the hardness of him pressing against my front the most perfect form of affection I'd ever been shown. A free giving. Uninhibited.

I hooked my ankle around the back of his knee to hold him tighter, and he lifted my leg higher around his hip, opening my thighs wide, the back of his cock grinding against my clit. My whimpers got lost in his mouth, but he lifted me before I could come again. My legs wrapped around his waist, and he held me beneath my thighs, pulling back enough to see my face.

My fingers clutched at the balled muscles of his shoulders as he lifted me even higher until his cock notched against my opening. Lips parted, sharing breath, Ricky lowered me, stretching me past the point of comfort, and I fought to keep from showing it on my face.

"Goddamn, you're tight," he said through clenched teeth, his brow furrowed.

I forced myself to relax although my fingernails dug into his skin at his thick invasion. Even soaked, my pussy made him work to stuff me full.

"Fuck, Casey." He hissed through grit teeth, and I finally let out a whimper as he shoved against my cervix. "Fuck."

That rippling energy between us snapped tight into alignment, and I lost myself in his eyes.

The bed met my back as he laid us down, the first drag of his dick pulling from my pussy clutching my heels and hands to keep him close.

"Not going anywhere, tiny dancer," he whispered against my lips, sinking back into me with one slow, slick shove.

"Oh, *fuck*." I arched beneath him, a rush of

arousal swelling through my torso and tingling every inch of my skin.

"This what you want?" Ricky half-moaned, pulling out again, the friction almost more than I could bear. "You want my dick?"

I pulled him back in, my groaned, "Yes," escaping as his ass flexed beneath my heels, burying himself again in one short thrust. "Holy fuck, yes."

"Look at me."

I hadn't realized I'd closed my eyes, caught up in the sensations running riot over and through me at his slow movements.

A hint of gold around his iris ... an even smaller hint of blue lost to the black of his pupils.

I'd only been with one man before—once—and he'd lasted all of five thrusts after taking the virginity I'd offered up just to have it over with already. I hadn't felt the need to connect with him beyond the physical so hadn't watched him fuck me for those twenty or so seconds.

Ricky stole my heart. Or had I given it already? Gone to the emotions swelling inside me, the need to hold him in my arms, I let go and rode the emotional waves, the ripples of energy between us.

He took my mouth gently as he fucked in and out of me, our bodies rocking together, hard and soft, seeming polar opposites that fit perfectly together.

This is only the beginning...

I'd gotten what I'd wanted all right, and nothing, no one, would tear us apart.

13

RICKY

*S*o tight.

I wondered over Casey being a virgin, but there was no fucking way a woman waited until their mid-twenties to give it up. The thought of being her first, her only, slammed a caveman-like feeling through me and I wanted it more than I wanted oxygen.

I tore my mouth off hers with a groan and sat back on my haunches, holding her thighs wide as fuck—limber as a goddamn gymnast. Dragging my dick out of her sopping core didn't reveal a tint of red, no blood.

Not a virgin, but fuck, did my dick stretch her little hole as I shoved back in. So pretty and pink—I wanted to fuck her raw. Make her cry and scratch the hell out of my back. She squeezed her inner muscles around me, and my eyes rolled back into my head.

"Goddamn, baby." Teeth grit, I pulled out and thrust in with more force. "You're so fucking tight. Feels like I'm your fucking first."

"I wish." She gasped as I hit her cervix, her back bowing off the bed. "Only once before—" She gasped as I thrust harder, on the verge of losing my shit.

Didn't need her talking about who had her pussy first. Fuck, no.

I hadn't fucked a woman in months, and even though I'd been blowing loads left and right every day since I'd first seen Casey, being inside her made me feel like a goddamn green teen, ready to bust a nut at first dip.

Lifting her hips gave my dick a deeper reach, and she grimaced when I thrust into her heat, balls deep. "Fuck—did I hurt you?"

"Feels good." She licked her lips and opened her eyes when I didn't move. "Too good."

Fuck that. "Never too good." I yanked her upward, my arms a vise around her tiny body. "Hold onto me."

Her nails shredded my back as I fucked into her, my mouth finding her neck, fucking biting when I should have been kissing. My fingers bruising when I should have been caressing. Couldn't fucking control myself.

So soft. So sweet. The whimpers and moans coming from her mouth like a soothing beam of early morning sun, piercing the darkness as I buried myself inside her over and over.

"Ricky," she breathed my name, her breath caught—and she shrieked, her pussy clenching at my thrusting length, sucking me deep, milking…

I shuddered at the first shot of cum shooting from my dick. "Fuck, Casey … Goddamnit. Fucking *hell*." A few other curses spewed from my mouth against her neck as I emptied my balls inside her pulsing pussy. Needing more, so damn swamped by her, I grasped her face in my hands and took her mouth, fighting for breath as the last shudder and spurt escaped me.

"Fuck, baby," I murmured against her mouth as she sagged against my chest, pliant as putty and sweaty as fuck.

Our hearts thrummed between our slick, heated bodies, our kisses turning leisurely as my dick softened. I couldn't set her aside. Didn't want to leave the warmth of her body, the cocoon of whatever it was wrapped around the two of us.

"I hurt you," I murmured, forcing myself to let her breathe.

Lips red and swollen curved upward as she smiled at me, her fingers rubbing up and down the back of my buzzed hair. Her tits, soft and lush squished against me, the blue of her eyes sated and sleepy. "Only a little."

"Sorry."

"Don't be." She dug her nails into my shoulders and clamped her legs tighter around my waist as I shifted to lift her off my dick. "It's just been a long time."

"How long?" I asked, not meaning to growl like a goddamn primal animal.

Her smile widened and she relaxed in my arms again, her thumb rubbing over my lower lip. "Four years."

"The fuck? Seriously?"

"Just the one time, too."

I blinked and studied her for a few seconds. "How old are you?"

"Twenty-six last month."

"And you've only had sex once?"

"Yep." She leaned up to nip my lower lip. "And he didn't even last a minute."

I snorted, feeling like thumping my chest. "One pump chump."

"More like five or six, but yeah."

"No wonder I fucking hurt you." My brow furrowed, but not out of guilt or pain. "You should have told me."

"If I had told you I was only this far removed from being a virgin," she said, holding up two fingers a hair apart, "you wouldn't have taken what I willingly offered."

"Fucking right." I let out a huff and rested my forehead against hers. "It's surprising any man has gotten inside your pants considering who your father is."

Her turn to snort. "Tell me about it. Only reason I even gave it up was because I was a freshman in college and had a chance to give it up without his knowing."

"You weren't in love with the guy?"

"Hell, no. He was simply an act of rebellion."

"Ha." I pulled back, and smirked at her. "So you admit you're rebellious."

"I was once upon a time," she said, snuggling closer against me, the drying sweat and stickiness of our bodies pressing tight.

A hint of insecurity trickled through my brain. "So am I another act of rebellion?"

She squeezed her pussy muscles, tugging on my softened dick. "Hell, no," she repeated with a grin. "You're the first man I've ever wanted to share myself with. The first to tempt me out of sheer fucking need."

Silence rose between us for a few moments, my heart still beating in my ears as we held each other's gazes without the need to look away when intimacy got to be too much. I'd only had that with one woman, and not nearly to the extent I did with Casey.

"Why me?" I finally asked her, my fingers trailing up and down her spine.

"You're protective, yet soft." She chewed on the inside of her lip, and I wished like fuck I could read her mind because I knew she had a shit ton more to say on the matter.

But unlike her, I wouldn't push. I'd take what I could get and tuck those precious memories away for when she realized I wasn't good enough for her.

14

CASEY

I wondered how much of the truth I could share without scaring him off. Men tended to be turned off by my forwardness, by my opinioned thoughts I usually didn't hesitate to share.

I'd had plenty of men declare they loved me, but it had always been for the outward, the idea of Casey Dawes, not the inner most parts of me, the pushy girl who fought tooth and nail for whatever she wanted. Would he freak the fuck out if I told him what I wanted? What drew me to him?

What held me back from suddenly being forward with Ricky when I usually had zero qualms about speaking my mind?

"I can hear your brain working," he said without

a hint of teasing. "Just say whatever is on your mind, tiny dancer. Don't hold back now. You've got nothing to fear."

Fear. That's definitely what had clamped my lips shut. The thought of losing the best thing I'd ever gotten my hands on scared the ever loving shit out of me.

"Fine." I inhaled until it hurt—praying my words wouldn't cause damage. "Your eyes are full of pain, and I have this driving need to fix everyone and everything."

"I can't be fixed. Too many broken pieces." He stated the words with finality, but still, he didn't set me aside, allowing me to study his face, allowing me to see his vulnerability. He also hadn't taken offense to my all but calling him damaged goods.

A step in the right direction.

"Will you stay?" I asked, not nearly ready to give him up for the night. "Give me the rest of tonight before taking off again?"

Ricky touched my hair, my cheek, then gently pressed his delicious lips against mine in a chaste kiss—lingering enough to warm me clear through. "I'll give you tonight."

———

Ricky carried me into the shower and washed me from head to toe, his touch reverent, every kiss he brushed over my skin like he wished to memorize the taste, the feel of me. God, how I soaked in his attention, my entire body stringing tight. It had to be close to two in the morning, but I hadn't had nearly enough.

I soaped him up good and sudsy, the caress of my hands turning the semi he sported from washing my body to hard as fuck and ready for another round.

"I want you again," I murmured against his chest, my body hot, wet, and swollen.

"It'll hurt."

I tilted my head back to look up at him. "Don't care."

"You'll care tomorrow when you have trouble walking."

Shit balls. The thought of an ache I'd never experienced before atop the slight one already between my thighs took me from needy to *fuck me right the fuck now*. "Let me ride you," I said, squeezing his dick with one hand and fondling his heavy balls with the other. "I'll stop if it's too much —just fucking need you again, Ricky."

He groaned, his forehead finding mine again, his hands reaching around me to grasp my ass. "Fuck."

He thrust into my hands, yanking me close. "You're not allowed to hate me in the morning, Casey."

"Promise." I stepped back and rinsed off quickly, hopping from the shower and grabbing two towels.

He chuckled behind me, and I tossed the towel in his face.

"Hurry the fuck up, boy toy. I need your dick again."

"Needy little vixen."

I stuck my tongue out at him, and his gaze darkened as he rubbed the towel over his head, his hair more auburn than blond when wet.

"How about I take that mouth instead?" he murmured, his eyes full of lust.

"After I fuck you."

"Goddamn, Casey." He growled and stalked after me as I scurried backward, laughing my ass off.

"On the bed." I said, sticking to one side to keep him from grabbing me and pushing me to my knees.

He eyed me, his blue eyes blazing, a hint of a smile on his mouth while lying back and tucking his hands behind his head.

Fuck, his body...

I would never tire of the sight. All rippling muscle, dips and valleys my tongue salivated over.

Mine for the taking.

Grinning, I climbed onto the bed, determined to claim him heart and soul, the same as he'd done to me.

134

15

RICKY

Lying still was the hardest fucking thing I'd ever done. Casey worshiped me from head to fucking toe, like I was a god, and she my faithful, loyal servant. Teeth, tongue, and lips, she tasted every inch of my chest and abs, her tongue salivating all over my fucking hips, my dick leaking and begging for more. She definitely had a thing for that V women always drooled over, lingering for far too long.

Finally—fucking finally, she flitted her tongue over the tip of my straining cock, lapping at the pre-cum her worship had enticed from my balls. My abs contracted as I curled upward, teeth clenched and fingers laced tight as fuck behind my head.

"Fucking tease, Casey. Suck my dick already."

Light laughter accompanied a quick glance up at my face—and she tilted my dick upward with one hand, her fingers cupping my balls. "I promised I would *after* fucking you"

"Please—"

Holding my gaze, she took me deep. So fucking deep...

"Holy *fuck*." I curled upward again and cursed harshly as she tongued the hell out of my length, the slight scrape of teeth, the softness of her fuckable lips... Fucking green Ricky reared his head again, and I grasped her shoulders, yanking her up to claim her mouth before I blew like a goddamn teenager. "Fuck me, Casey. Please—let me inside that tight pussy of yours again. Fucking please."

She notched herself, and I fought like fuck to keep from thrusting upward. With a hiss, she pressed back and stopped, shifted her hips a bit and tried again, stuffing another inch of me into her body.

"Need help," she whispered, and I slowly flexed when she moved back again. "Fuck, you're big."

My eyes rolled back into my head, and I clenched my teeth, trying like fuck to be gentle in helping her get her fill of my dick. Groaning, I clasped her face in my hands and kissed her, trembling, fucking shaking like hell.

Took her too damn long to rest her pussy lips against my groin—I was gonna fucking blow. "Move your hips, baby," I gasped against her mouth, and she started rocking. "Fuck." I reached between us, needing her clit. She bit my lower lip as I pinched her swollen nub. "Need you to come all over my dick, Casey. Fuck, I need you."

She shuddered, a low whine growing in her chest as I continued to play with her, cupping her pussy around my dick as she dragged herself off me and stuffed herself full again. My hand a soaked mess, I found her clit again and thrummed the fuck out of it, my other hand tangling in her hair.

"Come for me, baby."

Casey stiffened and shrieked, her pussy clamping down on me like a goddamn vise.

My balls exploded, and I swear to fucking Christ I passed right the fuck out. Gone to the world. Gone to reality. Gone to everything but Casey and her softness, her sweetness, her fucking lush as hell curves wrapped in my arms.

———

"So, what are you doing in Vegas?"

Loaded question.

We shared a pillow when we should have been passed the fuck out. I sure as hell wasn't proud of my past, so in typical Ricky form, I tossed out a half-truth. "Needed a new start." Wasn't really a lie.

"How come?"

Of course, she would ask.

I shrugged my shoulder not buried in her mattress and glanced away while considering lying. I'd already told her I had drinking issues, but she didn't need any more truth that would turn her away from me which probably would have been for the best anyway. Too bad I was a selfish, weak-assed fucker.

"Didn't feel I belonged there anymore," I again stated a half-truth. "My brother found his old lady, the other officers have settled down. A couple of them just had kids." I let out a heavy sigh, those truths arcing that ache through my chest again. "Sucked seeing everyone with stars in their eyes."

"Jealous?" Her blue eyes laughed even though she kept a straight face.

"Right at this moment, fuck no." I gathered Casey into my arms and pulled her close until our noses touched. "Haven't felt this good in a long fucking time, tiny dancer."

"You're going to stay until morning, right? No sneaking off?" she asked, tracing my lips with her fingertips.

"Promise not to tell your father?"

"Fuck." She scowled, dropping her fingers from my mouth. "You had to go and ruin the moment."

I shrugged again, but couldn't admit to self-sabotaging the good things I found in my life.

She let out a huff and snuggled close. "I'll take care of my dad."

Unless he got to me first...

I stayed. Woke first and enjoyed the gift of watching her eyelids flicker open, her blue eyed, sleepy gaze landing on my face and lighting up my insides with sunshine.

I fried up some eggs for our breakfast and drank down the best damn coffee I'd ever tasted. Keeping the shit of my past a secret, I shared what I could about my life back east. Didn't mention Annie. Didn't mention the demons, the lone grave of the bastard who'd spawned me and Vigil, the insecurities. She seemed to see past my half-truths, though, squeezing my fingers and once pulling my head against her chest when I broke up about losing Auntie Jeanie.

"I was always a mischievous little shit," I told her as we snuggled on the couch after our late breakfast. "Always getting into trouble. Devious. Sly…"

"And?" she pushed when I faded off, my thoughts toward how I behaved since meeting her: back to my old ways of wanting to lie to protect myself. Definitely an addict.

"And now I feel I'm going that route again," I admitted. "Lying to your dad. Sneaking around like a little shit wanting to get my dick wet regardless of rules set in place."

She snorted. "Some rules were meant to be broken."

"He placed them to keep you safe," I murmured, my fingers toying in her long hair.

"He doesn't know you." She snuggled against my chest, and I closed my eyes, breathing her in.

It was a good thing he didn't know me—but I wasn't about to speak that fact out loud. "Tell me about you. I'm done talking," I murmured against her hair.

She laughed and launched into the tale of Casey Lynn Dawes life. And I thought I'd been mischievous. I laughed at some of her childhood tales.

Snorted. Kissed her senseless when I couldn't handle how perfect she seemed. Fuck, even her stories lit the darkness in my life, the trouble she got into—far different from my own—quieted the howling demons I'd never been able to drown.

Light and life.

How the fuck would I live if she had her fill of my dick or found out the truth of my past before her father killed me?

I wouldn't. That grim thought followed me back to the hotel, and I punished myself for giving in and losing our damn bet, barely able to stumble into the shower after my workout.

16

CASEY

That inability to walk without remembering Ricky's dick? Yeah. Stinging soreness, and I couldn't keep the smug look off my face while sitting down to dinner with Mom and Daddy on Sunday afternoon.

Mom knew. Moms always knew, she'd assured me the first time I saw her after losing my virginity.

The second she saw my face when I'd walked into the kitchen, hers paled, and she kept her lips clamped shut. Ever the vigilant, know-it-all and see-it-all, Daddy should have known Ricky and I had been together, but he was a typical clueless man who went back to his football after we ate.

"If your father finds out," Mom whispered as we

stood side by side washing up the dishes, "he'll kill him."

"Ricky's a good man," I whispered back, for the first time a feisty protective bear like my dad.

"But he disobeyed your father's order to stay away from you!"

"Ricky is not Daddy's to order around," I argued back. "He's not a Vegas Viper. Daddy holds no sway over him."

"Still, he should honor your father's request. It's a matter of respect. As should you, young lady."

I rolled my eyes, feeling like a damn teenager all over again. "Why? I want him. He wants me. We're both consenting adults."

"It's the disrespect and dishonor I'm talking about." Mom's lips thinned as she rinsed a pot and handed it to me.

"Well, Daddy is wrong this time."

He wasn't usually, and Mom's side-eye let me know she thought the same.

"Please, just give him a chance," I urged as the thought Mom might break my trust to tell Daddy the truth. "Please. Let this play out as fate would have it."

"And if fate would have me tell David the truth of what you're doing in order to protect you from that man's past?"

"What has Daddy learned?" I asked, my heart creeping up my throat at Mom's insinuation.

"He's a drunk, Casey. An addict."

"He told me that already."

"Did he tell you he's been one for twenty years and only sober the last month or so?"

"No, but that fact doesn't bother me. We all have demons. We all try to run from them. He's sober now and maybe having a good woman by his side will help him stay that way."

"And if it doesn't?"

My throat tightened, but I wasn't about to give up on the man I felt sure I'd been born to stand beside. "Then I'll hold his hand and help see him through his darkness."

"Some men can't be healed, baby."

Mom's whisper tightened my throat to the point I fought to voice my thoughts. "But every man should be given the chance and the caring support to try. You've said Daddy was a mess when you first met, and he's right as rain now from what I can tell."

She didn't respond, and I didn't know if I'd pleaded my case successfully.

"Time will tell," she whispered while hugging me goodbye an hour later. "But please guard your heart." At least she hadn't said anything to my father while I'd been with them.

That "time" she spoke of wasted away with me doing my daily hunt for a job I'd taken up the week before. With med school out of the picture for the immediate future, I needed something more than dancing to keep me busy. Idle hands and all that shit.

God knew Ricky wasn't interested in keeping me as busy as I'd hoped. He texted back every time I reached out. We spoke on the phone for hours on end—but he refused to come see me or fuck me.

Guess his one taste of me hadn't been enough to keep our secret affair ongoing.

I imagined he feared my dad finding out. He claimed he didn't.

"Tell me you're not suddenly needing to honor my father," I griped on Thursday night over the phone after getting home from dancing my ass off to a bunch of salivating, cat-calling assholes.

"Not really."

My brow furrowed when he didn't elaborate, and I considered the face I had memorized, the emotions he sometimes had allowed me to see in his eyes. "It's guilt, isn't it?" I asked as the thought lit in my head.

"You're feeling guilty for not honoring my father even though he isn't your superior."

"Maybe a little."

"And?" I pushed, feeling like a snippy, little yapping dog with teeth sharp enough to rip and tear until I got answers.

He let out a heavy exhale. "Guilt has made itself a permanent home in my head and heart, Casey. Been living with that shit for over twenty years. Kinda hard to keep my head above it, but I'm trying."

"You don't have to obey my father. You're not a Viper."

Ricky held his silence for long enough I realized I might have overstepped.

"Sorry," I murmured, letting out a sigh. "I know I'm pushy—I just really want to help you. I want my dad to chill the fuck out and allow me true independence for once."

"He's only trying to protect his little girl."

"I can protect myself," I grumbled, hating I sounded like a brat, but unable to help myself.

Ricky chuckled, and the sound twitched my lips. "I'm sure you can."

"So when will I see you again?" Pushy. Yeah. Couldn't stop the need to be with him. Wasn't just his dick, either, although I certainly missed that part of him. "It doesn't hurt to walk anymore," I said, closing my eyes and imagining him creating that sting again. "I'm forgetting what your dick feels like inside me."

"Damnit, Casey."

"All stretched out. Filled." Arousal spread clear through my body.

"Fuck."

"Hard for me?" I asked, sassy as ever and smirking.

"Always."

"So come on over here and let me take care of you."

He didn't answer.

I let out an annoyed huff of air. "Can we at least take this to a video chat so I can watch you masturbate?"

Ricky groaned.

And I got my way, the sight of his hand griping his leaking dick between that V of muscles the hottest damn thing I'd ever seen. Afterward, we stayed on the phone until my eyes crossed from exhaustion.

I hated saying goodnight over a cell rather than

in person, but at least I drifted off to dreams about falling asleep right where I wanted to—in his arms, safe and secure.

17

RICKY

Why the fuck couldn't I tell guilt to fuck off so I could live my life however I wanted beat the hell outta me. Casey was everything. Couldn't stop thinking about her. Dreaming about her—her laughter, her softness, her body I'd lost myself in.

But the two times I'd stopped by the Vipers' club after work that week, Butcher eyed me as though he knew I'd fucked his daughter and bided his time to take me out. Being who he was in the club, I expected he'd gotten the dirt on me. If not through Klingon, then someone back home. Couldn't blame the man, though. If I had a daughter, I'd want her to steer clear from the likes of me, too.

Fucking depressing.

At least I didn't go looking for a bottle.

I looked for apartments instead and found something a few blocks from the club. Spent all day Saturday moving what little shit I had into the place, thankful the one-bedroom came furnished. Wasn't much, but the central AC and a shower was really all I cared about.

I bought and set up a new weight set in the living room's corner, then beat the hell out of my body that night to keep from going to see Casey dance.

Sunday, gun exchange day, and I didn't question my wanting to help the Vegas chapter. Even though I hadn't accepted Klingon's invitation to join their club, I felt I'd made some friends, and all but Butcher continued to welcome me like I belonged. Temptation to join warred with loyalty to Vigil and the brothers back home.

But I'd ruined that when I'd left even if my brother claimed he held my colors for me.

Tension ran high as the Vipers met at the club Sunday at nine. Silence reigned over the group as Klingon laid out the plans for the second time that week, his attention to detail and ability to hold his men's attention made him one hell of a president. He didn't have to take any shit because his men knew better than to dish it out.

Respect. Those boys had a lot of it—and I tended toward the same.

Klingon clasped my shoulder as we filed out into the night to load up into the three vehicles headed to the warehouse where shit was going to go down. "I appreciate you."

Three words that meant the fucking world to me. My father hadn't ever said them, only my big brother—and not nearly enough to build up the insecure little punk I'd been. I nodded and climbed into the SUV beside him.

The punk gang had agreed to all Leftie set up for the exchange, having no demands of their own. Stupid idiots. They had no fucking clue who they dealt with. Way over their fucking heads.

We arrived at the rundown industrial park an hour prior to the sale, and we took up our spots spread around the cavernous building—some inside, some out. I ended up closest to Butcher, not surprisingly. He would want to keep an eye on me. We sat hunkered by another abandoned building, closest to the road. My ability with a gun making me the last man standing between whatever punks escaped and the open road.

Leftie's men would leave out the back with the cash, and the Vipers inside would hopefully take down all the interlopers. Any stragglers who managed to escape back out the way they'd come in, wouldn't get past the five guns hunkered outside, including Prophet atop the building at my back with his sniper rifle.

Every single gun had a silencer attached. We hoped to make as little racket as possible and slip back onto the highway without issue.

Silence stifled while we waited, but at least the heat had relented with the hiding of the sun. Stars expanded off into the distance overlooking the desert beyond us, the lack of moon making for a fucking dark as hell night.

Spotlights from the warehouse's corners shone down in some areas, creating deeper shadows beyond where the Vipers hid.

A cargo van pulled into the parking area to my right a few minutes after midnight, tires crunching on the broken up black top. Eight guys, exactly as Prophet had stated, hopped out the second the vehicle stopped, bandanas around their foreheads, their pants sagging halfway down their asses.

Stupid kids must not have listened when their parents told them if you mess with fire, you get burned.

Ten minutes we sat once they went into the

warehouse, my breath loud in my ears, not even able to hear the murmur of voices from those inside. Sweat dripped down my back in a lazy path, and I fought to ignore the droplet trailing down my temple.

A couple of pops sounded, and I tensed, breath held, gun in hand, ready to hop up if any of the fuckers made it outside.

The warehouse's door flew open with a bang, and two of the punks spilled into the night, one with a bloody shoulder, the other doubled over and stumbling, the front of his wife-beater soaked with blood. Two quick pops from behind us, and the men fell, Prophet's powerful rifle's punch sprawling them back against the warehouse wall.

An engine roared to life, and I jerked my focus toward their van—someone sat behind the wheel. Must have been in the back—

Being the closest, I hopped up, gun in both hands, aimed, and squeezed off a shot as the van jolted into motion. Fucking missed.

I shot again but couldn't clearly see the driver as he careened like a madman, trying to turn the truck and get the hell out. A few other muffled pops sounded—the tires blew out, and the vehicle came barreling for where Butcher and I stood side by side.

The loud bark of a handgun exploded, shattering the windshield.

Butcher shouted a curse.

More shots—the driver shot at us, making a break for the freedom beyond us.

I held still, holding the wild-eyed driver in my sites. Breathing deeply. Waiting for him to get closer...

Pop!

My bullet found its mark between the fucker's eyes. He slumped forward, the van turning slightly, on target to flatten me.

"Move!" I shouted, sprinting a few feet to the side. I dove, taking Butcher down with me, the crunch of metal and shattering of glass exploding against the abandoned building in my ears as we hit the dirt, Casey's dad on top of me.

Fuck.

My ears rang, and pain twitched in my back.

"You okay?" I grunted, rolling Butcher's bulk off me.

"Hit."

"Fuck." I rolled him to his back, and yanked my t-shirt off overhead to press to the oozing wound on his shoulder.

His lips in a grimace, he closed his eyes, brow

furrowing.

I glanced back at the warehouse to see Klingon emerge from the door like the fucking grim reaper, dressed all in black. He put an extra bullet into each of the downed men sprawled where his sniper had landed them. Turning, his head swiveled back and forth as though checking out the scene outside of the warehouse.

Pennies approached from the opposite side of the road leading into the area, and made doubly sure the driver of the van wouldn't move again even though I'd plastered his brains against the head rest.

I flagged down Klingon. "Butcher's down. Shoulder."

Klingon stalked toward us in the night, a hulk of a man blending into the shadows. No teeth flashed, but I could make out the concern in his eyes as he dropped to his knees beside me.

"How bad?" he asked Butcher.

"Shot through. I'll be fine," he answered through grit teeth.

Klingon nodded dend helped me pull Butcher up to his feet. "Let's get the fuck outta here."

Two Vipers' vans we'd left a few hundred yards down the road approached, their headlights off.

Cleaners.

Without a word, I helped Butcher into the SUV while Klingon stayed back to make sure the mess got cleaned up.

A man I didn't recognize exited the warehouse. Dark suit, button down shirt—but no tie. Klingon shook his hand before slapping his shoulder. Figuring it was Leftie, I turned back to Butcher to make sure he was okay.

He fumbled with his cell.

"Let me help," I said, holding my hand out.

Butcher eyed me for a few seconds before handing it over. "Call Janet. Speed dial 2. Let her know I took a bullet but that I'm fine. She'll fucking kill me if I don't."

"She knew about tonight?" I asked while swiping his cell's screen open.

He grunted and shifted on the seat beside me. "She knows more than she should, yeah."

So I wasn't the only bastard who chose to bend club rules a little.

I did as told, not questioning his telling his old lady about club business. Wasn't *my* business. Making sure he felt comfortable and the shoulder stopped bleeding was my business. I would see him safely back to the club.

"Thank you."

"For?" I asked, handing him his phone back after hanging up from my ten second conversation with Janet.

"Saving my life and killing the fucker who shot me."

I nodded. "Anytime."

A truthful statement made without an ulterior motive. Maybe the fresh start in Vegas *was* making me a better man.

18

CASEY

Mom called me around one in the morning. Daddy had been shot and was on his way to the club—but that's all she knew.

Not giving a shit about club business or what I was/wasn't allowed to know, all of hell couldn't keep me from heading over to make sure for myself that he was okay. God knew the Vipers wouldn't send him to a hospital to get patched up. They would call in whoever they had in their back pocket.

I barreled past Pennies to get through the club's door, and my father's cursing could be heard through the entire place, easing the twisting in my stomach. Mom stood by the hallway leading back to the extra rooms I knew some of the brothers rented, her face pale.

"How is he?" I asked, grabbing her into my arms for a quick hug.

"He'll be fine. Shot through the shoulder, so he'll be sore for a while. I expect he'll belly ache quite a bit until he heals, too."

I let out a shaky laugh, the weight smothering my shoulders relenting. Only the two of us knew how much Daddy hated pain. God forbid when he got splinters or stubbed his toe. Big badass? Yeah. Until he got a little boo boo.

"Are you okay?" I asked her, and she nodded, swiping a tear from the corner of her eye. "Can we go back to see him?"

Mom clasped my hand in hers and led me back the hallway toward the rooms set aside for brothers who didn't have a place to crash.

The doc finished with the stitches by the time we walked into the room and he nodded at Mom, starting to give her instructions on how to care for the wound once they got home.

I hurried to his side, scowling. "The hell were you doing? You're an old man. The younger brothers should have taken care of whatever you meddled with."

Daddy grimaced up at me from his chair as I crossed my arms.

The doc continued to drone on while Mom picked up the shirt that had been cut off my father. A pile of bloody rags strewn on the bed stand beside him.

"You okay?" I asked, my frown easing, my voice lowering. I tended toward anger when loved ones got hurt.

"Be fine, pumpkin."

Lips tight, I nodded—and a tingle raced over my skin. Mouth suddenly dry, I glanced over my shoulder.

Ricky stood in the doorway in a pair of black jeans, his torso bare and gorgeously ripped.

Shit balls, my heart.

Our gazes snagged, and I couldn't look away. His eyes... The desire found there suggested he wanted to pull me into his arms and comfort me. My feet itched to take me toward him.

"Ricky saved me." My dad's declaration jerked my attention back toward him. Was there a hint of respect in his voice?

"Good thing he lwas with you," I replied, not bothering to hide my satisfied smirk.

Daddy nodded, lips tight as though he'd said enough good about the man behind me. God forbid

I take his words as a green light to get what I wanted. They did give me hope, though.

I brushed Daddy's hair back, leaned in, and gave his forehead a quick peck. "Glad you're okay. I thought for sure I was going to puke on my way over here."

He chuckled, brushing off my concern with a, "It's no big deal," when he knew I hated to puke as much as he liked pain.

But it was. Daddy wasn't getting any younger, and if anything happened to him, Mom would follow on his heels into the grave from a broken heart. Without the two of them, I would have nothing. No grandparents left and no first cousins I knew beyond names and the fact they lived in Kansas somewhere.

The fragility of life crashed into me as I stared down at my father, choking me up, but I refused to show weakness.

"Be right back," I murmured and slipped past Ricky without making eye contact, intent on the bathroom and privacy for a few minutes.

I clutched the sink, head lowered as tears dripped and I fought to keep from losing my shit.

In my whole life, Daddy hadn't been injured even though his lifestyle certainly could have landed him six feet under at any time. I'd lived a blessed life. How often we became familiar with the blessings we have and forget to count them.

He's alive. He's fine. "Maybe Mom will talk some sense into his stubborn ass and tell him to take it easy," I grumbled to myself.

One last shuddered breath, and I splashed water on my face. A handful of scratchy paper towels worked to dry off my face, and I eyed myself in the mirror that needed cleaned. Zero makeup. A hint of dark circles under my eyes. I looked and felt exhausted. I also wanted nothing more than to fall back into bed and allow Ricky to hold me like I felt sure he wanted to do.

God, did I need him.

He stood outside the bathroom door when I exited. That look in his eyes again...

Without a word, we fell into one another, a heavy sigh releasing from me at the warmth of his chest against my cheek. All tension, all concern for my father, and fear I could have lost him, dissipated. Ricky's heart thrummed beneath my ear. Closing my eyes, I breathed in the scent of his skin, my fingers clutching at his bare back.

I'd never tended toward depression or wallowed in despair, but Ricky was my moon, lighting up the darkness in my night. The thought of losing him twisted my stomach anew.

"Are you okay?" I asked, pulling away enough to see his face.

"Yeah." He smoothed back my hair, his thumb lingering on my cheek in a mindless caress.

"Not hurt at all?"

"No."

I closed my eyes on a silent prayer. "And the man who shot my father?"

"Paid with his life for trying to take out my brother."

My eyelids snapped back open. "Your doing?"

"Yes."

I should have been horrified by Ricky's lack of hesitancy to reply or regret in his eyes, but pure satisfaction coursed through me. My man had saved my father—and exacted revenge on the man who had tried to take *his brother's* life. "Thank you."

"Gotta admit, didn't do it for you in that moment," he said quietly, his gaze searching my face. "Came natural, like fate put me there."

I smiled and lifted onto my tiptoes to breathe against his lips, my heart warming to know that I had pegged him as a good man even if Daddy didn't. "Glad to hear it."

Ricky closed the distance between us, his lips soft and yielding when I'd expected hunger. Didn't men who faced death need to fuck the adrenaline out of their system? God knew my body leapt aboard that train in two seconds flat.

His arms wrapped me tight, every hard inch of his body against my front. Arousal, thick and toe-tingling flooded through me.

"Come home with me," I said against his mouth, completely melted into his embrace.

He hesitated. *Not a no...*

I kissed him again, rubbing against him like a cat in heat.

"Casey Lynn Dawes!" Daddy's bark jerked me back, but Ricky's stepping away from me severed our contact completely, leaving me cold.

Red filled my father's face, and I swallowed, my chin rising even though I longed to wrap my arms around myself.

"Thought I told you to steer clear, young lady."

"Thought he just saved your life," I shot back even though I recognized the bullheaded stubbornness in Daddy's eyes. There would be no talking to the man.

Ricky had selflessly saved my father and not to please him or prove what kind of man he was. His instincts to protect should have been what my father focused on, exactly as I'd done.

I shouldn't have been surprised Daddy chose not to.

Mom stood beside him, their hands firmly clasped, her lips zipped shut.

I shouldn't have been surprised by their united front, either.

19

RICKY

"You're not good enough for her." Butcher turned his focus on me as I stood, hands fisted at my sides, my insides jittery and flaming with fucking need to bury myself inside of Casey and disappear for a few hours.

Fuck, how I wanted to lie. Make excuses and place blame on others to make my past look squeaky clean, but I wanted that fresh start. Wanted to keep the new man I'd found in Vegas. That meant being honest with Butcher—and myself.

"I know I'm not good enough," I stated quietly, flicking my gaze at her stubborn face. "She deserves the world, and I can't lay it at her feet."

Her eyes softened, searing my chest with pain.

Without another word, I spun and walked away,

the silence of the three I'd left behind worse than the shrieking demons at my heels, trying to once more drown me with emotion.

The club's door slammed shut behind me, but opened again as I strode across the dark parking lot, my focus on my truck and getting the hell out of there.

"Ricky!" Klingon called after me, his tone worried.

I didn't stop.

Ten minutes later, I sat in front of a liquor store even though they didn't open for quite a few hours. My hands gripped the steering wheel as I stared at the dark interior.

So damn thirsty.

Those demons howled through my head, ringing and echoing, whispers tempting me to break a window and take what the fuck I salivated for.

Not good enough.

Never measure up.

You should have been the one to die, not Annie.

The image of her blue-hued face flashed through my mind, seizing my heart before slamming the fucking thing back into high gear without squeezing the clutch. I grasped at my chest, teeth clenched, and stare hazing.

Annie is gone. My fault.

Both truths I'd admitted to myself hundreds of times, but I'd never offered myself forgiveness no matter how many therapists insisted I do so. The self-bitterness had ruined every relationship in my life, the one with my brother included.

I'll only bring her down...

And yet another truth.

I thought I'd found my place, but the sudden floundering threw my goddamn mind for a loop. Fuck, how I wanted to do the right thing, and falling into Casey was pure weakness. She was the wrong choice because being with her went against honor—to Annie, to Butcher, and his old lady. Never mind the truth her father had spoken about me.

While I'd come to appreciate Casey's independence and strength, she didn't need me. Wouldn't ever in the way I wanted a woman to need me.

I fucked up by giving into lust. Fucked up by wanting to comfort her in that one moment of weakness she'd shown.

Lesson learned, karma, you bitch.

Thanking fuck the liquor store wasn't open to truly tempt me into spiraling down into that damn rabbit hole again, I backed out and returned to my apartment.

20

CASEY

My heart ached at Ricky's slouched shoulders, but I bit my tongue to keep from calling him back to me. He either didn't want to fight for me or was cowed beneath the demons of the past enough that he felt he didn't have the right to stand at my side.

"I thought I told you to stay away from him!" Daddy lit into me the second the club's door slammed shut behind Ricky.

I spun back around, anger flaring to life inside me, heating my face. "I'm twenty-six for fuck's sake! It's time you let me live my own life!"

His glare didn't waver, and Mom didn't say a word. "I let you dance. Gave in on that, but I want what's best for you from here on out."

"Maybe Ricky *is* what's best for me," I snipped back.

"Leave it alone."

"I won't, Daddy. I want him. I find myself looking at him like Mom watches you."

Daddy's eyebrows lessened their scowl, and his hitched shoulders eased even though the movement must have hurt his injury. "I've noticed, but you don't know him," he insisted.

"Then let me *get* to know him," I pushed, proud of myself for not whining like I wanted to. "He's not intimidated by my personality *or* you. I can't say that about any guy I thought I might like enough to bring around."

We stared at one another, but with less bull-headed pissiness between us.

"He didn't save your life for me, you know," I continued, grasping at straws. "He told me it was instinct to protect his brother."

Daddy didn't blink, but I caught the heartbeat of uncertainty in his eyes. "Addicts lie at every turn. It's not just something they can turn off."

"And some people learn the extent of their inner strength by going through trials."

His lips pursed again.

"David," Mom murmured. Not a plea, but not

said in manipulation, either. Simply a request for him to reconsider, and tears stung my eyes again. Mom never went against him.

"I'm not giving my blessing for you to pursue this thing, but I won't stop you, either," Daddy finally said with a grunted exhale. "But don't come crying to us when that man breaks your heart."

My chin lifted again in desire to have Ricky's back even as a tingle of excitement swept through me at Daddy laying off. "What makes you think he will?"

"He has demons."

I'd heard that one already. "Don't we all?" I reminded him. God knew Daddy didn't have a squeaky clean past.

"Some don't relent and tuck tail for hell again, pumpkin. They'll cling stubborn as fuck until the poor soul dies."

Daddy knew that to be truth, too. I'd heard whispers about club business between him and Mom. I knew he carried around regret for some of the choices he'd made as the Sergeant at Arms and a one-percenter. I also knew he'd held more than one brothers' hand while they slipped into eternal darkness.

"Maybe not," I said, "but sometimes all it takes is

having someone to help hold your head above water to keep those demons from drowning you." I glanced at Mom and back to him again, reminding him of his own past.

Daddy dipped his head in acknowledgment of my statement, and they turned for the door as one, leaving me to follow along behind.

Given the green light.

"Thank you, Daddy," I called to him over the top of my car as Mom helped him into his truck's passenger seat.

"Please be careful."

My smile probably lit up the goddamn parking lot as I hopped into my car. The call I put through to Ricky the second I settled in the driver seat went straight to voice mail.

"Goddamnit."

I hated having my plans thwarted.

He told me he'd found a place to rent, but not the address.

Lips tight, I shot off a text, telling him to call me, but if he had his cell turned off, he wouldn't see the damn message.

Going home to my empty house sucked big balls —unwashed, hairy ones, but I didn't have a choice.

21

RICKY

A new man meant a new life, and even with the woman I longed for off limits, I couldn't leave Vegas. Just being near her would have to be enough. I would be the shadow keeping her safe even if she didn't know I lurked.

Determined to remain on the straight and narrow path I'd chosen, I knew I needed to make things right. Klingon gave me the address I requested, and I found myself knocking on Butcher's door later that afternoon.

His old lady answered, but didn't seem the slightest bit surprised to see me standing on their stoop. "Come on in, Ricky. David's resting in the living room."

"How's he doing?" I asked, following her into

their home, breathing easier in the AC's coolness. Vegas might be my new home, but the heat would take some getting used to.

"He's sore." She glanced up at me with a glint in her blue eyes Casey had inherited. "Grumpy, too," she whispered. "But I think he'll be glad you stopped by."

I nodded and followed her into the living room.

Butcher sprawled in a recliner, his bandaged arm in a sling, remnants of a sandwich and a glass of ice water on the small table beside him. His face held zero trace of reaction at seeing me which was a hell of a lot better than the pissiness I'd expected.

"Hurting?" I asked, nodding toward his shoulder.

"A bit."

"Why don't you sit down, Ricky," Janet said, motioning toward the couch. "I'll get you something to drink."

"I'd appreciate it. Thank you."

I settled, but kept my ass on the cushion's edge, elbows on my knees and hands clasped. "I wanted to apologize for not honoring your wishes."

"Casey is hard to resist," Butcher grumbled, and I bit back my smirk.

"She's a breath of fresh air," I said, my chest aching. "Like a beam of sunshine."

"Especially to a dark soul."

"Yes, sir." I nodded, glancing down at my hands. "But my devious days are over. I'm sober and have every intention of staying that way. Going back to the life I lived before would mean death, and I refuse to give into that weakness. I refuse to wallow in the shit or allow the howling demons to drown my soul."

I met his gaze head on, not in hope of changing his mind about Casey and me hooking up, but that he would accept me as a brother. Without his blessing, I wouldn't ever fit in with the Vegas chapter, something I realized the night before I truly wanted.

"I would give my life to keep Casey safe," I continued, "same as I did for you, but not because I want anything in return. Yeah, I've made a hell of a lot of mistakes over the years, but in this, I'm going to do what's right. She's like a bright as fuck flame, and I'm a moth caught in the magic of her, but I'm hell bent on honoring her father."

Butcher stared at me, and silence settled as Janet returned with a glass of ice water for me. She settled on the recliner's arm, her hand entwining with Butcher's hand on his uninjured side.

"I appreciate the honesty, Ricky," he finally said after I chugged half the water down, the tension twisting my stomach eased a bit at having part of what I wanted to say out in the open. "Our daughter wants you—no doubt about it. Anyone with eyes can see the way you look at one another."

Janet smiled softly, glancing at Butcher's profile.

He let out a heavy exhale, his lips pursed for a brief moment. "If she is what you want, be her friend first. Get to know her. She's a lot of woman. A stubborn, rebellious brat."

"I'd say independent," I countered. "And it's easy to see where she gets it from."

Butcher snorted a chuckle, surprising the hell out of me, his eyes taking on a twinkle of real laughter. "You don't pull any punches, do you, brother?"

Brother. Warmth spread through me, and I found my lips rising in response. "No, sir."

"A quality I appreciate in a man." Butcher's smile faded and he nodded. "You got any past demons I need to fear rising up to hurt the club or my precious girl?"

The rest of the shit I needed to spill...

"Just the ones inside me. Feelings of inadequacy. All others have been buried, but I'll give you the details if that's what you need to give me a shot with the Vegas Chapter."

Butcher shook his head. "No need to stir up shit that's been laid to rest if there's no trace."

Vigil and I had left bones behind deep in the woods of Maine, but not anywhere someone would stumble upon. Our bastard of a father had disappeared not long after beating our mom to death, and no one seemed to give a shit.

"I think it's safe to say there's no evidence to lead back to me."

"Good." He eyed me, but I didn't shift under his inspection. "She's going to want to hold your hand and heal you. If that's not what you want, then walk away right now."

"Are you telling me I can pursue her, Butcher?"

"Fuck knows I can't keep the two of you away from one another—just do as I said. Be her friend. Make sure she's the kind of woman you need beside you in life before getting all caught up in the emotions."

That had already happened on my end, but I wasn't about to admit to fucking his daughter and losing my goddamn mind over her. "I will."

"Try to tame my girl, and I burn you down," Janet said, jerking my focus off her husband.

I bit back my laugh at the seriousness, the stubbornness in her face. "Casey didn't have a chance at being meek and quiet, did she?" I couldn't help but question.

Janet's lips twitched and Butcher chuckled again.

"There's a bit of bullheadedness in the family, can't deny that," Butcher said. "Makes for hella good fights and even better make ups."

Pink stained Janet's cheeks as Butcher squeezed her hand and held her gaze.

To have a love like that...

I cleared my throat and stood. "I appreciate you seeing me."

Butcher made to stand, but I held up my hand. "Stay. You look comfortable as hell."

"Could use another pain killer," he muttered, and Janet hopped off the recliner's arm to go get the medicine bottle the doc had given him at the club.

"Just take it easy," I said, noting it wasn't a simple bottle of over the counter pain meds. "That shit is addictive as hell."

"You speak from experience." Butcher popped the pill, his gaze on me.

I nodded. "Learned a hard lesson because of it, too. Paid with a life I valued more than my own."

Butcher didn't pry, simply nodded. "Slow and easy," he reminded me.

"Yes, sir."

I would honor that request, but decided to start immediately rather than wait any longer. Feeling lighter than I had in years, I cranked the AC in my truck and headed toward Casey's. Butcher had brought hope, but would his daughter still want me after learning the shit of my past? While her dad didn't need details, I felt Casey deserved to know everything. All of it, nothing spared. I wouldn't lie to her. Wouldn't hide the truth of what had shaped me into the man I'd become and the man I wanted to be.

There would be honesty between us—or nothing at all.

22

CASEY

My man was not the one I expected to see at my door right before dinner. I hadn't showered. Hadn't done my hair beyond a ponytail. No makeup prettied my face, either.

Ricky still looked at me like I was a goddess, the emotion in his eyes snagging my breath.

"Hey," I said, pulling my door open wider. "What are you doing here?"

"Wanted to talk."

I'd already stepped back to let him pass, and he did, the scent of soap and Ricky assaulting my body from sniffing nose to tingling toes. A shiver slid over me as I shut the door behind him.

"Death wish?" I tossed out with a laugh while locking up.

"Got your father's approval to be your friend."

I turned and stared, but couldn't find a hint of joking etched in his face. "Shut the fuck up."

"No. Seriously." His slow smirk sent my lady bits to heaven in a needy kind of way.

"Get your ass in here and tell me every word."

He followed me into the living room and sat on the couch. I curled up on his lap without hesitation.

"So, friends, huh?" Sweeping my fingertips over his addictive lips, I went for full-on sassy, horny siren. "Like the fuck buddies sort?"

Shit balls, that smirk...

"Didn't get the go ahead to bang Butcher's hot as fuck daughter, no, but he's not totally against us taking it slow."

"Slow sucks." I pouted.

The hard length against my thigh suggested he agreed, but he stopped me from closing the distance between our mouths. I raised an eyebrow in question.

"We need to talk."

"Okay, so talk," I said.

Ricky shifted me on his lap—away from his hard dick, his focus dropping to my thigh he caressed. "I'm not a good man," he started, and I held my tongue knowing he had some shit to spill. "My father beat my mother to death. My brother and I returned the favor and buried the fucker deep in the woods of Maine."

I laced my fingers with his that lay on my thigh, unmoving. He continued to avoid my gaze.

"While he deserved what he got, I couldn't help but feel guilty. Started drinking at a young age. Got hooked on heroine when I was seventeen."

Silence settled, and I sat quietly, giving him time to gather his thoughts.

I didn't need to know the shit of his past, it meant no difference to me and wouldn't change how I felt about him, but part of helping someone heal is listening. Allowing them to unload and carrying some of the burden for them.

I would do it a million times over if it meant a future for us like Daddy and Mom shared.

"Had a girlfriend." Ricky's voice broke, and he cleared his throat.

Her. I squeezed his hands a little tighter, my eyes stinging at the pain on his face and etched in his voice.

"Her name was Annie." More silence as his jaw worked. "She was shy. Quiet." He swallowed, his own voice barely more than a whisper. "She was the clingy sort, couldn't do anything without me, and I soaked that shit in. I'd never known adoration like that. Even our mom hadn't been the affectionate sort."

He trailed off as though he was caught up in memories, and I ran my hand along his jaw and to the back of his head, my fingers running over the buzzed hair.

"Tell me what happened, Ricky."

"Annie always looked after me whenever I got drunk or high. Always sat with me. Held my hand. Made sure I didn't hurt myself."

Heavy silence swelled once more, and I barely breathed beneath the weight of guilt I could feel radiating off him.

"I was fucking high as a kite. Can hardly remember." Ricky shifted me on his lap, his brow furrowed and eyes closing as he tipped his head back against the couch. I settled my hand on his shoulder and waited.

"Talked her into getting high with me. Just the once. I wanted her flying alongside me."

The furrow in his brow spoke volumes. I could guess at what had happened.

"I tell myself every time I see her face that it

wasn't my fault, that she made the decision on her own, but Annie loved me to the point of an unhealthy addiction. She did whatever I asked. And if I hadn't been fucked up..."

Kiss him? Hug him?

I chewed on the inside of my lip, unsure of how to help him. What to say. What to do.

"For twenty years I've been running from my demons. Tried to drown them before they could do the same to me. Thought it would be better for everyone if I was dead, too. I didn't deserve life when the love of mine no longer breathed. I suffered for the pain I caused—still do if I think too long on what I've lost."

Ricky's brow twitched, his frown deeper, his lips pressed tight.

"I'm a fucking mess inside, Casey." Finally, he opened his eyes, allowed me to see the pain, the regret, and guilt eating away at his soul. "Don't think I deserve to be happy when I see all my brothers with their old ladies on their laps, but fuck if I can keep from being drawn toward you. You're a ray of sunlight reaching through the darkness inside me. I should suffer for all the pain I've caused, but you make me want to find happiness again. Scares the shit out of me."

"Why?"

"What if I fuck up again? What if I make another mistake and can't protect you from the festering inside me? What if I drive you away by my wrong decisions and I'm left alone again? Can't fucking do it, Casey."

"My father isn't your favorite person, right?"

His brow furrowed again. "What?"

"And yet you threw yourself in harm's way in order to save his life."

Ricky didn't reply.

"How many times have you saved one of your brothers' lives back home? You've got a natural protective instinct. There's no way my father was the first. Am I right?"

A hundred thoughts seemed to flash over his eyes while I waited. "Yeah," he finally answered.

"Did you learn your lesson about doing drugs, Ricky? Have you ever even considered shooting or snorting again?"

"Never. Stuck to booze after that day."

I cupped his cheek, so desperate to get through to him my throat tightened. "You made a mistake. A costly one. But it was her decision, not yours. You didn't make her do it. Didn't hold a gun to her head and give her that ultimatum." I knew whatever I said wouldn't snap him out of his grief or heal him in a flash, but I hoped in time he would find freedom.

"You've been running for a long time," I said, my voice quiet as I caressed his whiskers under my thumb. "How about you turn and face the fuckers trying to suck the life out of you? How about you allow me to hold your hand and help shoulder the burden?"

"I don't want to drag you down."

"You won't," I stated with absolute assurance. "I'm a stubborn bitch. I know how to stand on my own two feet."

A shadow flitted over his eyes.

"What?"

Lips tight, he shook his head, glancing away again.

"Talk to me, Ricky."

"That's the thing—you're capable of living life without a man beside you. You're strong as fuck, independent with a capital fucking I."

And once again, my inner strength makes me undesirable. I'm not like her, *I'm not what he wants.*

My throat tightened. How many times had a guy decided I was too much? How many were intimidated by my being too much of a woman?

"Everyone has needs," I managed to whisper.

A wry smirk lifted the corner of his lips, and he focused on my eyes again as though wanting to peer deep into my soul seeking out my needs. "As much as I'd love to fulfill *those* needs of yours, I promised your father I would take things slow. Be your friend."

I hadn't been talking about the physical, but I wasn't ready to correct him and dive headfirst into my own insecurities. Talking about them wasn't something that came easy for me. I hated stating my weaknesses and failures. Felt that cemented them more strongly in my heart. Gave karma and fate something to play with.

"We'll be friends, then, if that's how it needs to be," I whispered. *For now.* "Hungry? I was going to grill some chicken."

"Chicken's good." His smile, the relief in his eyes soothed me like a warm blanket on a rare, cool night.

I knew I could get pushy when I wanted something, but Ricky desired to honor my father. Doing so would make him feel better about himself. I wanted him happy. Wanted him to feel he'd made right decisions in earning us.

Even though I longed to press my lips to his in a chaste, soft kiss, I refrained and slid off his lap. "Come on. You can make the salads."

"I'm not a rabbit."

I laughed and tugged his hand, pulling him into the kitchen behind me. "Well, if you're sitting at my table, you're eating whatever the hell I put in front of you."

"Yes, ma'am."

23

RICKY

Casey didn't show once ounce of judgement toward me. Didn't send me packing after unleashing my demons on her. Didn't look at me with disgust knowing I'd killed my own father and was responsible for Annie's death, a complete innocent whose life had unfortunately crossed with mine.

Her soft touch proclaimed the exact opposite of judgement. Her eyes stated she accepted my past for what it was, that she still wanted me.

Wanted, not needed.

My heart stung at that truth, but the desire to lose myself in her—kiss her mouth, have every inch of her skin against mine, bury myself in her warmth until I no longer felt alone... Casey had somehow managed to dig her claws deep inside me.

I'm fucking gone on her.

She didn't let me help set the table. She didn't let me help with the dishes.

Casey Dawes didn't need me, but she'd given me the desire to prove I could be a good man. She gave me the desire to strive for a better Ricky, and not just in my outward choices. I wanted to be a better man on the inside. Find my own strength and learn how to deal with my insecurities.

She wasn't what I thought I wanted, but she's what *I* needed. In one hell of a short fucking time, she'd become the center of my universe. Scary as fuck. Probably too fast and too fucking dangerous. But I'd allowed myself to be vulnerable. She held my heart in her hands, and I feared the unintentional shattering to come.

Even though there was a connection between us that couldn't be denied, something lacked, and I knew I could never make Casey need me in the way I wanted her to. Trying to force it, control her in any way, would blow to hell any chance of a future.

But could I live without the kind of love I longed for? Could I survive without feeling appreciated? Needed like air?

I didn't kiss her goodnight. Didn't even pull her into my arms and soak in her sweet scent and soft curves. She allowed me to honor her father's wishes —and I couldn't decide if I loved or hated that fact.

24

CASEY

His insecurities held him back. I could see it in his eyes, and while I normally wouldn't have that and push until I got what I wanted, I needed to give him time and space to realize we were good together.

Opening up and spilling like he had probably would have gone a long way in creating a bridge to span the gap that had sprung between us, but I would find a way to get around having to show weakness.

I always did.

The fact I wasn't good enough, wasn't what he thought he wanted, devastated me, but I'd sunk my teeth in like a pit bull and wasn't about to let go. I just needed the chance to show him that we were good together. His softness to my hardness. My giving nature for his hurting and the neediness of the good kind he seemed to portray. Giving him the adoration and affection he seemed to crave fulfilled me in ways I'd never dreamed—and I hadn't had nearly enough, nor had I given enough.

The need in Ricky's eyes turned me on more than any man's touch ever had. I became addicted to him. Wanted to feel him beside me. Wanted his eyes on me. I wanted to be the center of his world. I wanted his thoughts, his dreams—I wanted to own his heart in the way Annie had.

But she'd been needy. Clingy. Exactly the type of woman he seemed to want.

I couldn't even pretend to be that sort.

We spoke on the phone every night that week, and he came to watch me dance Thursday and Friday, staying until I got off for the night and taking me home—with Daddy's permission. He didn't touch me other than holding my hand while driving. Didn't kiss me after walking me to my door. No sexual innuendos. No accepting my invite to come inside although his eyes said he wanted inside—in more ways than one.

Saturday he sat in the dark corner for both of my sets, his stare and our lack of physical affection creating a tension so tight inside my body that I wanted to scream—both in frustration and euphoria, his name on my lips for both.

I needed to get laid—that is what anyone would say who spent more than five minutes in my company.

Ricky seemed on edge, too, his lips in a thin line when I opened his truck door for myself.

Sorry I can't be your little maiden who can't do a damn thing on her own.

I was smart enough to keep the thought to myself.

Add in my inability to land a job or even a call back for a second interview, and pissy became my middle name. Ricky being the smart man he was, choose to keep quiet. Not poke the bear inside my body's cage.

"You okay?" he finally asked while pulling into my neighborhood.

"Fine." I stared out the passenger window, arms crossed.

"Seem a bit more than just sexually frustrated."

I didn't want to talk about the fact I couldn't find a job on my own. Hated that if I got my daddy involved, I'd be working by Monday in a medical office of my choice. I'd finally earned my independence from him and his hold, and I loved that freedom to just be me and choose what I wanted.

I would stand on my own two feet.

"Don't want to talk about it," I snipped, hating that my throat tightened.

"You don't have to be strong all the time, Casey," Ricky said quietly, reaching for my hand. When I didn't unwind my arms from around my center, he settled his hand on my thigh and gently squeezed. "It's okay to be vulnerable and need someone."

His words clanged around in my head for a few seconds, my stomach tightening to the point of pain.

"That *is* what this is about, isn't it?" I asked, the shit starting to spew before I could bite my tongue. "The fact I don't need you like Annie did? I'll never be clingy or say I can't live without you because I can."

You'd think I sucked all the oxygen out of the cab of Ricky's truck. We barely breathed, and I cursed myself for being a fool as he pulled into my driveway and put the truck into park.

He didn't speak, and a quick glance at him revealed a clenched jaw and flared nostrils.

I didn't know how to take the words back. Didn't know what to do but open the door and slide out. "Thank you for the ride," I choked out, and he backed up before I could move away, the truck's door slamming shut on its own.

Shit. Stupid bitch...

Tears welled and dripped off my chin by the time I locked myself inside the house. I told him I could live without him—but I didn't *want* to. Why hadn't I told him that part? What had held me back?

Without showering, I laid on my bed, hating the insecurity of not knowing, of not being able to control my future.

First med school, now my love life...

I was confident and independent, no doubt, but I was also insecure, spoiled by an overprotective father, and allowed childish reactions in my emotions rather than thinking before replying.

Without doubt, I ruined whatever chance I had with Ricky. I'd shown exactly how unlike I was his precious lover from the past. I would never compare to her. Would never be good enough for the man I thought fate had set in my path.

Sleep wouldn't come, and instead of calling him and spilling all the shit of my own life, I chose the coward's way out. Perhaps I didn't want him as much as I thought? If that were true, then the agonizing ache in my chest and heart didn't make sense.

Sunday night, my night off, and I finally found the guts to text Ricky, asking if we could talk. He texted back about an hour later letting me know he hung at the club with Klingon. We would have to connect later.

Jealousy was an ugly bitch, but I couldn't help her green, snake-like slithering through my brain.

My cell chirped two hours later while I stared at the TV screen, and I grabbed it off the coffee table hoping to see his name.

Skin Tight. Talk about a hope fader.

"What's up?" I asked, knowing why he called—the only reason he ever called.

"Two girls didn't show up. Can you come in?"

I had nothing better to do other than wallow in self-pity and pissiness, so I agreed. Wasn't like I'd been invested in the Grey's Anatomy rerun. "I'll get there as soon as I can."

Since Ricky had been my ride the previous two nights, I considered calling him—but he was at the *club* with his brothers. Yes, I definitely sneered at the thought. He couldn't be bothered to even talk to me, never mind give me a ride.

I called my babysitter, but he didn't answer. Probably sat alongside Ricky. While my dad didn't like me driving to and from work alone, it couldn't be helped.

Dancing without Ricky watching hadn't changed—it was still a bore, a damn chore. I didn't take one bit of joy out of it. My skin actually crawled as other men hooted their approval, their lustful gazes sending shivers of the non-enjoyable sort over me. My second set of the night couldn't end fast enough.

Ricky hadn't called me. Was he getting drunk off his ass because I'd hurt him? Had I caused him to fall back in line with what his demons wanted for him?

I felt like shit inside and out. My heart ached. Bags clung under my eyes even though I'd managed to cover them with makeup.

Skin Tight saw me to my car, but I still kept my gaze scanning the parking lot as my dad had taught me. A shiver of a different sort slid over me, and not the kind that let me know Ricky watched. My arm hairs stood on end as a tingle swept up my spine.

"Are you alright?" Skin Tight asked as we approached my car.

I looked into the darkened cars close by but didn't see anyone lurking about. "Yeah. Just feeling spooked for some strange reason."

"You seemed a little off tonight. Trouble in paradise?"

I hit the unlock button on my keychain, the queen of bullshit rising. "Everything's good."

"Want me to follow you home?"

"I appreciate the offer, but no." I focused on my boss and smiled. He would never understand what it was like being the daughter of a one-percenter who probably had unknown enemies out the ass. Always needing to be on alert pounded into my brain since I'd learned how to talk. "I'll be fine."

"I appreciate you coming in tonight. Could tell your heart wasn't it in, though. At least the guys didn't seem to notice."

I snorted while climbing into my car. "As long as the ass and tits are shaking, they don't give a fuck what a woman's thinking or feeling."

"Not all men," he said with a laugh and shut the door behind me. "Be careful," he mouthed, and I started my car and waved, noting him in my rearview watch me until I turned onto the ramp leading to the highway.

Going home to an empty house sucked ass. Going home while knowing Ricky hadn't even texted or tried calling me sucked ten times worse. Like a green jolly giant unshaved ass worse. One that hadn't been washed in a week.

At least I made myself chuckle at that visual even though my chest felt caved in on itself.

I dug my keys from my purse while climbing up my front stairs.

A quiet rustle of clothing sounded, and I started to spin. Sharp pain smashed through my temple, and I crumbled beneath the blackness rushing toward me.

25

RICKY

I sat at a table with the Viper officers, sipping a tonic while they drank their beer. For a Sunday night, the club had grown rowdy, music blasting and whores making their rounds. Butcher sat on my left, his arm still in a sling, but the tension that had been between us no longer lingered. He'd clasped my shoulder in greeting, calling me brother.

Even though Casey's last words to me had crushed my heart, I still found myself relaxing, proud of myself for going straight to my apartment the night before rather than hit a liquor store.

She'd said she could live without me.

I should have gone straight to the bottle—but I hadn't, and I felt fucking good for it.

Why hadn't I ever appreciated being sober

before? How had I ever thought being off kilter and half out of my mind was better? I loved the clarity of thought to work through what Casey might be going through, and why she'd lashed out at me like she had.

She'd meant every word, and even though my heart still stung from that nasty jab, I found the strength to be a man. Hold steady.

She texted asking to talk, but I wasn't going to be jerked around by her emotions when I had enough shit of my own to set straight. Her pissy attitude could wait, so I told her I'd call her later.

Sitting back in my chair, I watched the club around me, feeling like I was finding my place. No demons whispered in my head. No guilt ate at my insides.

Klingon knocked his fist on the table, drawing everyone's attention. He nodded toward his office, and like a herd of sheep, we all stood and followed, me being the last when he stated, "You, too, Ricky."

I closed the door behind me, shutting out the ruckus of the club.

The officers stood in a half-circle facing me, and I pulled up short, eyeing them one by one, unease tingling down my spine.

Klingon picked up a leather cut off his desk and tossed it to me.

I held it up, eyeing the colors for a few seconds before turning my attention on him.

"I put it before the officers even though it's a club law abiding transfer," Klingon said. "We're in agreement that this is where you belong, Ricky. I spoke with Vigil. I know there's no loyalty issues between you and the Boston Chapter."

Leaving as I'd done, though, should have put me on a blacklist, unable to gain any Vipers' trust. I'd never been more thankful for my brother. For friends—*brothers*.

"Put it on, kid."

Kid. I kept from snorting and did as told, settling the leather over my t-shirt. The weight of the cut felt right, and I straightened, holding his stare and not bothering to hold back my grin.

"Welcome home, brother." Klingon moved in and hugged the hell out of me, no bro side-hug bullshit.

Goddamn. My eyes stung as he slapped my back. Felt fucking good.

Each of the officers said the same, but offering handshakes—except for Pennies. He hugged me like

Klingon had, ruffling my hair like he was the elder of us two.

Still grinning, I accepted their congratulations, and we went back into the club, Klingon's shout dropping the noise to a minimum.

"Welcome our new brother, boys!" he hollered, and that sense of finding where I belonged settled in stone.

While the others celebrated with shots and beer, I made do with a can of pink lemonade.

———

I got home late as fuck and crashed, knowing I needed to be up in four hours to get my ass to work. Fucking Mondays—even not hung over, dragging my ass out of bed sucked a big one. I didn't even have time to grab a coffee.

I shot off a text to Casey while sitting at a red light, asking if we could get together after I got off work. Knowing she had two interviews lined up for later that day, I told her I'd be thinking of her. Best of luck and all that shit.

She hadn't texted back by lunch break, so I tried calling.

No answer.

I had trouble focusing on work, but told myself she was either back to being pissy or was still caught up in an interview.

Once I packed up my tools for the day, I tried her again, my stomach knotting when she still didn't answer. I never got a text about how her interviews went, either.

A sense of unease put me on alert, and I questioned the pissiness being the reason she didn't respond. I put a call through to Klingon for Butcher's number, not bothering to worry my new president with something as silly as a woman not answering her phone.

Butcher didn't answer my call, but I texted letting him know it was me since I doubted he'd programmed my number when I'd never given it to him.

He returned my call seconds later. "What's up, brother?"

"You hear from Casey at all today?"

"No." He clipped the word short, and I knew he felt the same sudden anxiety I did.

"Has Janet?" I asked.

"Janet!" Butcher's holler sounded muffled. "You talk to Casey today?"

I couldn't make out her answer, but Butcher

swore in my ear a second later. "Do you know if she had any plans after her interviews today?" he asked me as I fought off rising nausea.

"Nothing, and her second interview was at one. Definitely should have been done by now."

"I don't want to be that overprotective father, but something doesn't feel right," he muttered.

"I'm feeling the same," I said, changing course for Casey's. "I'm heading over to her house. I'll call you when I get there."

I hung up and gripped the steering wheel tight as fuck, my concern rising to the point I couldn't keep from speeding and hollering at other drivers to get the fuck outta my way.

Her car sat in the driveway, and a rush of breath left me. Parking behind her, I eyed the house and pulled blinds. I hopped out of my truck and strode up the walkway, steeling myself for the little chat we needed to have.

Her cell phone lay on the stoop, her purse a few feet beyond.

"Fuck." I pounded on the door and hollered her name, but the door didn't open. "Casey!" I tried again, ready to kick the fucking door down. My hands shook as I rifled through her purse. No keys. "Casey!" My fist hurt like fuck from smashing it against the door.

Her cell and purse looked like she'd been attacked from behind... I searched the ground beside the stoop—her keys lay half-buried by a shoe print that was way too fucking big to be hers.

"Fuck." My hands shook as I let myself into her house, but there was no trace of her. No appearance of a struggle. I grabbed my cell from my back pocket and rang Butcher.

"She's gone," I rasped, my stomach twisted to fuck, my mind focused on finding her and killing the fucker who thought to take what was mine.

Balboa had also gotten a call from Casey the night before, letting him know she'd gotten called into work. Since he hadn't answered, she said she'd just drive herself over to the lounge.

I cursed myself to hell and back again for not calling her back.

A call through to the strip club let me know Skin Tight had seen her safely to her car and watched her get onto the highway. None of the other dancers noted anything or anyone strange the night before.

The local hospitals didn't have anyone matching Casey's description in their care.

She'd never made it to either interview she'd lined up.

I stalked a path across Klingon's office while a tear-stained Janet clung to Butcher's hand. Both were pale as fuck. Balboa and the other officers had gone out to comb the fucking streets, but night fell and we still couldn't find her. No answers. No hint of what the fuck had happened.

I'd never felt such a sense of helplessness, even when Annie's chest had refused to rise on its own while I'd sobbed over her body, attempting CPR. Absolute fucking hopelessness. Hands fucking tied. Zero answers.

Fuck, the need for whiskey burned my throat, and I fisted my hands, telling myself to make my woman proud.

My cell buzzed, and I pulled it out, Balboa's name I'd entered in just hours before popping up. "Tell me you've got something," I shot the second I swiped to answer.

"Neighbor's got one of those camera door bells."

I held my breath and pulled up short, my focus on Butcher and Janet.

"Casey got home at two-thirty," Balboa said.

"Fucker in black clobbered her upside the head and carried her off camera."

"Fuck!" I squeezed my eyes shut. "Other neighbors along the street got cameras?"

"Nothing."

"No car, no plates?"

"Nothing."

"Fuck." I hung up and shared the news. Janet sobbed, but Butcher held my stare, his face blank. Did he blame me for his daughter's disappearance? Did he think someone from my past had come gunning for me and took her to hurt me?

"If it was intended as payback, we would have gotten a call by now," Klingon noted from where he sat behind his desk. He watched Butcher. "I'll make some calls. Spread the word. See what we can stir up."

Butcher nodded, the first hint of pain crossing over his face.

I needed to take a fucking walk and stalked to the bathroom, splashing cold water on my face to help me focus. Rage flared inside me like a goddamn flame thrower, searing every cell inside my body. Burning me the fuck down.

Someone had taken my woman. Fucking stole her because I hadn't been around to keep her safe.

Fuck going slow. Fuck being friends first. I should have been with her regardless of her pissiness and lashing out at me for whatever shit she had going on in her head. I should have been beside her, watching her dance, crawling into her bed with her every goddamn night.

I peered at myself in the mirror, my hands gripping the sink. Blood-shot eyes stared back at me, but I hardened my gaze to shut off all emotion.

Gotta stay sharp, I told myself. *Stay in the goddamn game and go find your woman.*

"Ricky!" Klingon's holler jerked me away from the mirror, and I strode back into the club. He stood in his office doorway, cell in hand, dark eyes thunderous.

I moved quickly, shutting us back inside his office.

He handed me his phone, Janet's sobs twisting my guts back into tight knots.

The image on his cell stole my breath, and I locked my knees to keep from falling to them.

My sweet Casey lay trussed up like a pig, blindfolded, lips slack around a ball gag. Naked and bruised to hell.

Realizing it was a still from a video, I hit the play arrow, fighting to keep from puking my guts up.

She didn't move, but the camera did, a man's heavy breath the only sound as he rounded her still body. At least the hint of her chest moving indicated she breathed.

"You want this feisty cunt back," the man said, his voice muffled but unable to hide a Latino accent, "then return the guns we paid for."

"Fuck." I grit my teeth as he lowered the camera closer to her face.

One of her eyes swelled from beneath the blindfold, and blood mixed with the saliva around the black ball stuffed into her mouth.

"You have twelve hours to drop the shipment at the same spot you gunned down my boys. The second you clear out, I'll call to let you know where she is. Try to cross us again, and we'll find another tasty Viper morsel to steal from beneath your noses."

The video feed cut out, and I looked at Butcher. "Didn't you say those fuckers had a safe house somewhere close by?"

His eyes lit. "Estes Ave."

"Fuck." Klingon put through a call, his gaze on my face. "Balboa—yeah. We got word someone from that gang of pricks we thought we'd wiped out has her. Get your ass over to that big ass blue house on Estes Ave, but don't make a move until we get there."

"Klingon?" I held up a hand.

"Hold on, Balboa—what?" he asked me, pulling his cell away from his mouth.

"Isn't Estes Ave close to downtown? Lots of eyes and ears? We go in there with our guns blazing, and we might draw unwanted attention."

"What's on your mind, Ricky?"

I glanced between Butcher and Klingon. "This prick's not looking to set up a direct exchange. We'll need two teams. One for the safe house, one for the warehouse. Drop a fake ass shipment and make the call. They'll probably only have a couple of guys on Casey—team one goes in quiet as fuck and gets her. Those fuckers show up at the warehouse, and we end this shit once and for all."

Klingon glanced at Butcher who nodded his agreement.

"It's a good half hour drive from downtown to the warehouse," Butcher said, "so you'd have to wait to go in to get my daughter. Wait at least until they get to the warehouse."

"The second those fuckers park their vehicles, you go in to get her," Klingon told me.

"And if Casey isn't there?" Janet asked, her voice

still choked by tears.

"Then we keep one of the gang members alive and get answers." Butcher's tone sent a shiver down my spine. I expected whoever the fuck we snagged with a beating heart would wish for death before sunrise.

Klingon nodded. "Balboa," he said into his cell, "scope the safe house out but stay out of sight. I'll send some men your way."

"You won't shut me out getting justice this time," Janet said, her chin rising as Klingon hung up.

"Shh." Butcher soothed her, but she wouldn't be quieted.

"That fucker hurt my girl, David."

"I know, baby." Butcher tucked her head against his chest with his good arm, his gaze on me. "But you and I aren't going."

"Yes, I am!" She tried to push away from him, but he held her tight.

"Ricky's going to go get his girl and bring her back to us, aren't you, brother?"

I nodded, lips tight. *Fucking right.*

"I'm trusting you to get the job done since I can't."

The coveted trust of one Butcher Dawes.

If I fucked up, we would all pay the price.

26

CASEY

A jab of pain in my side dragged me from darkness, and I moaned against my gag as awareness of pain throughout my entire body rose with consciousness. Fuck, did I ache. Cracked ribs for sure, I remembered while trying to take shallow breaths through my busted nose, the scent of stale cigarettes churning my stomach.

Ricky...

I choked back a sob and shivered against the chill seeping into me through the rough cement floor beneath me. How long had I been tied up without clothes? Was Ricky looking for me? Did he care I'd disappeared?

Daddy would, which meant the Vipers would as well.

Another jab to my backside had me twisting to escape his boot, and I groaned from the swift movements of jerking away from him.

Goddamnit!

The fucker untied the ball gag and it fell away, and I worked my jaw even though pain from having his fists smashed against it stung my eyes. "Why are you doing this?" I asked, my voice ragged as hell. I expected he'd stay tight-lipped same as the other times I'd asked him before he beat the hell out of me.

"Your father is a Viper and he messed with ours." He had a distinct Latino accent and didn't sound any older than my age. And as far as I'd heard and felt since he'd kidnapped me, there weren't a lot of men with him. But I couldn't know for sure since the damn blindfold had been tied tight as fuck around my head since the first time I'd been slapped to consciousness.

Did he and his tiny army think they could take on the Vicious Vipers MC and live to tell about it? I snorted even though it hurt like hell and my heart wasn't really in it. "And you signed your own death wish by messing with one of theirs," I tossed out acting brave even though I shivered and balked inside, my heart aching for

Ricky. "Kill me, free me, your end will be the same."

Fear had cinched tight around my chest the first time I'd woken and got to enjoy his fists and boots, and while it hadn't dwindled in the least, I refused to be cowed by the asshole.

"When they come for me, they're going to tear you limb from limb—after crushing your fingers and toes one by one. Wouldn't surprise me if they peel off your skin, too. Heard about that happening once." I grinned like a maniac even though confidence slipped through my fingers like grains of salt. "They hooked the guy up to an IV and kept him alive just so they could satisfy their desire for revenge for whatever his poor soul had done."

"*Puta perra.*" A fist smashed into my temple, but I didn't black out.

Whimpering, I laid still, breathing through the pain ringing between my ears. I spoke like a confident cocky bitch, but my insides didn't match my words. Would Daddy and his brothers come to my rescue? Would Ricky?

I expected I'd ruined my chance with him by refusing to be vulnerable, but I needed my man to come riding in on his white horse and save my ass. I needed his arms around me. Needed his love, his words, and tender touch.

Another kick tore my breath from my lungs, ripping Ricky's whispered name from my lips.

27

RICKY

Every second we waited ate at my stomach like acid. My insides fucking burned, rage to go berserk barely controlled by a thin rein.

The blue house sat dark, but the top of the line ear piece in my ear filled with Balboa's voice letting me know a dark shadow moved past a back window.

Klingon and a dozen other men, including Prophet, had set up at the warehouse after finding it deserted, ready for war. Then, he'd had a couple boys drive in with a van and unload the box of rocks.

He'd made the call.

I already sat a couple blocks from the safe house, night vision goggles in place, when three punks climbed into the box truck sitting in the driveway.

Balboa had approached the house from the back and sat waiting for me.

Waiting...

I hit the mic button on my chest. "Klingon, they're three guys in a dark box truck. Old as shit—heading your way now."

"We're ready," Klingon's muffled voice replied in my ear.

Going in too soon could alert those en route to the warehouse. Going in too late could mean a tip off to the ones watching my girl. We had eyes on the road going into the warehouse, and I waited for the whisper in my ear telling me the truck approached.

My stomach clenched tight like a vise, twisting tighter with every passing minute. We'd opted to wait for full-on fucking dark to cover our asses before calling in the exchange, so the neighborhood sat quiet.

At fifteen minutes out, I pulled off the goggles, climbed from my truck, and started up the sidewalk, my shoulders hunched inside my sweatshirt and hood pulled up. One gun tucked in the back of my jeans, the other in a shoulder holster. I also carried two knives—one at my hip, one in my boot.

I passed the safe house, checking it out in my

periphery. "Balboa?" I asked, pressing into the mic on my shoulder.

"Only the one guy—and he's disappeared," his voice came in quiet but clear.

Waiting...

The sound of a dog barking a couple blocks away and the hum of noise on the strip reached me, but nothing other than my quiet footfalls rose from the neighborhood around me.

Most people slept, and I didn't encounter any issues circling back and sneaking closer from shadow to shadow.

It seemed they'd only left one man behind with Casey, and watching the life fade from his eyes would be my responsibility. My pleasure. I'd already stated such and got no argument from Balboa.

I advanced like a wraith through the night, settling alongside a scraggly bush beside the front door. Lock pick in hand, I sat ready, adrenaline racing and heart thumping. It'd been years since I'd picked a lock, but I didn't want to go crashing through the door and giving the fucker a chance to make a call or grab Casey to hold her hostage.

Vigil and I had been sneaky fuckers in our youth, devious little brats enthralled with our father's gun cabinet. That had been the beginning of breaking and entering for us. Things escaladed from there.

I wished I was more like Vigil and could shut off my nerves and mind. Just get shit done.

"Got them in sight," Prophet said in my ear, and I slipped onto the porch, thankful for my steady hand.

"Balboa?" I asked while shimmying with the old lock.

"Got nothing."

Fuck. He could be right inside the door, fucking watching me. I could walk straight into an ambush, but I wasn't afraid of losing my life in order to save Casey's.

I'm doing it right this time.

Stone cold sober. No shifty or devious means, but straight the fuck in, gun up, and ready.

The lock clicked, and I grasped the door's handle. "Going in," I whispered into my mic.

28

CASEY

My kidnapper toed me awake again, and I bit back a moan against the damn pain. At least the fucker hadn't gagged me.

"Wake up you cunt. It's almost trade time."

Trade time?

I groaned and shifted, the rough concrete scraping against my thigh. Fuck, was I cold.

"Guess you were the right tasty morsel to take—they agreed to our trade. My boys are on their way to get our guns, and while I'm supposed to slit your throat before leaving, I think I want a taste first."

"Fuck you," I managed to rasp through the sharp pains in my ribs.

"Oh, I'm going to—cunt and ass."

My ass clenched on its own, and the sudden

need to pee almost overwhelmed my bladder. "They'll gut you—it's only a matter of time."

"We've got men, too, Casey Dawes. A new gang, and we've got big guns, too. No one steals from us and gets away with it. We're going to make a name for ourselves."

Bragging about big guns. He probably had a three-inch pencil dick. Knowing I would soon find out for myself churned my stomach, enticing bile to rise up the back of my throat.

"Yeah." I swallowed against the need to puke, my eyes stinging behind the blindfold. "By being the morons who thought to cross the Vipers."

"They crossed us first, *puta perra*."

Obviously Daddy and his brothers had stolen something from the Latino prick about to rape me.

"Because they own this town and needed to teach your stupid asses a lesson," I shot back, feigning the confidence I usually had in reserve.

He sat quiet for a time, and I strained my ears, my heightened breaths loud in the stillness. What did he wait for? My skin pebbled from the cold, and I swallowed again, determined to keep from puking my guts up.

"You could let me go," I said, my voice smaller

than I'd hoped for. "I haven't seen your face. I have no fucking clue who you are."

Nothing.

"You're getting what you wanted in exchange for my life—why not just give me back to them like you promised? You mentioned a trade. I'm assuming me for the guns?"

"Gotta teach those fuckers a lesson," my kidnapper finally muttered. "The call came through, the drop has been made. Once my boys let me know it's done, *you're* done."

I wanted to lash out, promise him I would be the last piece of ass he got, but fucking despair got the best of me. How much time did I have? Ten seconds? Two minutes?

"Please let me go," I whispered, thinking of everything I would never get a chance at life. Ricky. A baby of my own someday. A real job attained on my own. "I can't end life a failure."

"Spoiled little white girl—you don't know what a fucking failed life means."

He's so wrong... Showgirl. Med school. Ricky...

A tingle inched its way up my spine, the sweet shiver that warmed my skin. The memory of Ricky's eyes flashed through my mind, and the thought I would never feel his gentle touch again thickened my throat.

"I'm not the type of woman he wants long term," I whispered to myself, trying to make the loss of him easier to bear in my final moments.

"The fuck you talking about?"

Wetness leaked from my eyes and soaking into the blindfold again. "He wants shy, quiet, and clingy."

My kidnapper laughed, rippling goosebumps over my skin. "You're the fucking opposite." His voice came closer, his shoes scuffing the floor near my head. "A loudmouthed cunt, but I'll fuck the fight right out of you."

I shied as he brushed hair off my forehead and choked back a sob as my inner strength I'd always been so damn proud of ran off with its tail between its legs.

"I'm not good enough for Ricky," I whispered my insecurities out loud, knowing fate didn't give a shit about my life anymore. At least I'd had the chance to admit to them.

29

RICKY

I snuck back the hallway, the murmur of voices drawing me deeper into the safe house's interior. The second I recognized Casey's voice, a rush of air left my lungs.

Alive.

A door stood open, light spilling into the dark hallway in a rectangle of hope amidst the grungy carpet.

"I'm not the type of woman he wants long term." Casey's quiet voice reached my ears.

My brow furrowed, my palms around my Glock sweaty as fuck as I stopped, my back against the wall.

"He wants shy, quiet, and clingy." Her voice caught, and I realized she wasn't trying to play the fucker—she believed her words and the truth she'd concluded cut her deep.

"You're the fucking opposite." The Latino fucker.

The muscle in my jaw ticked.

"A loudmouthed cunt, but I'll fuck the fight right out of you."

I peeked around the corner, barely holding my rage in check. Couldn't go in like a goddamn blazing gun...

A dark haired guy crouched beside Casey, brushing her hair off her forehead. He didn't have a gun on him that I could see.

"I'm not good enough for Ricky," she whispered, and my heart fucking broke.

I tucked my gun in the back of my jeans and rounded the corner into the room. "You're wrong."

The kid leaped to his feet, pulling a huge ass knife from his hip, his dark eyes doing a quick assessment of my open hands held up in surrender.

"Ricky?" Casey's voice caught, but I kept my focus on the fucker—a fucking twenty-something kid who thought he could touch what belonged to me.

"You're everything I never knew I wanted or needed, Casey," I told her, my voice firm, my attention riveted on her kidnapper. "You're fucking perfection, baby. My sunlight. My reason for breathing."

She sobbed.

I took two steps into the room, and the kid stepped back rather than grab my woman and put the knife to her throat.

Big fucking mistake.

He blinked and licked his lip, glancing toward the open doorway behind me.

Yellow fucker.

"Your boys are all dead," I told him what Klingon had whispered in my ear seconds earlier as I'd crossed the house's foyer, and he gulped, tensed to make a break for the door.

This scared little punk will eat up my lies like candy.

I didn't take my focus off his crazed eyes. "You're the only fucker left, and I'd hate to kill you. Don't need any more blood on my hands."

"What are you saying, man?" he asked, the knife in his hand shaking as much as his voice.

"Why don't you straighten your ass out? Make better choices. Start the fuck over." I didn't move my hands, but took another step forward. "Give me that knife and get out of here before I change my mind."

Casey held still, my smart little vixen, trying to

choke back her sobs as her kidnapper and I stared at one another.

"Seriously gonna let me go?" he asked, his knife lowering to his side.

"Just hand over that knife so I know you won't hurt either of us on your way out, and we'll forget all about this shit," I promised. "Casey's alive—that's all I care about."

Big fucking lie.

He stepped forward, his gaze wary. "It's my *Papi's* knife."

I nodded and lowered both my hands to my sides, my legs tensing. "Then just get the fuck outta here, kid. Run and don't ever look back."

He glanced toward the door, and I sprang forward, grasping his wrist tight and jerking him forward. I pulled my knife from my side and stabbed it into his sternum in a smooth dance with death.

His mouth dropped open, and I stared into his eyes as he realized I'd ended him. "Y-you..."

I twisted the knife and yanked it back out, the teeth along its back ripping the little shit apart and spilling blood to the floor between us.

"I *lied*," I finished his sentence. "I believe in second chances, but not this time, you stupid fuck.

You hurt my woman. There's no fucking forgiveness for that kind of disrespect."

I released my hold on his wrist, and he slumped to his knees, dropping his *Papi's* knife to grasp his chest. One shove of my boot sent him toppling backward.

"Ricky?" Casey's ragged whisper dropped me to my knees, and I yanked my sweatshirt off, inwardly cursing at the close up view of her battered body. I draped it over her torso and pulled the blindfold off her head.

Bloodshot blue eyes met mine, slamming emotion into my chest. "You saved me."

"Would give my fucking life for you," I swore the truth in my heart while cutting the ropes off her wrists.

"Thought I wasn't good enough for you," she whispered, and I gently lifted her against my chest.

"You're *too* good for me," I managed through the tightness in my chest. "I don't fucking deserve you."

"I'm sorry." She clung to me and sobbed "So fucking sorry for everything I—"

"Shh." I stood and tucked her head against my shoulder. "Don't give a fuck about any past shit. We're starting over, Casey. You aren't going anywhere without me. Fuck going slow. You're mine, and no one, your daddy included, is going to keep me away from you."

"He's got her," Balboa said from behind us—I hadn't even heard the fucker sneak in. I knew he spoke into his mic, letting the other brothers know Casey was safe.

"I need you to take me home, Ricky," she whispered against my neck. "Need you to keep that promise and hold me every night. I need your smiles." She kissed my skin. "Need your frowns. Need you to challenge me, help me to become a better person."

The air whooshed right the fuck outta my lungs, and fucking tears stung my eyes.

"You've got every fucking piece of me, baby, and I'm never letting go."

30

CASEY

My parents stood on my stoop when we pulled up, the Vipers' doctor with them. Mom rushed to Ricky's truck to help me out.

She fussed with my seatbelt, her hands shaking. "Are you okay, Casey?" Her voice caught on a sob, and I laid my hand over hers, stopping her.

"I'm going to be fine. They didn't hurt me beyond what you can see."

"Oh, thank fuck." Tears streamed down her cheeks, and she looked like she wanted to hug me but didn't want to hurt me.

"Janet." Ricky's low tone had her moving away from the passenger door she'd wrenched open, and she stepped into Daddy's arms who stood on her other side, his lips in a thin line, his brow furrowed.

Ricky pulled me out of his truck, and I bit my tongue to keep from groaning, closing my eyes and laying my head on his chest.

A few minutes later, I laid on my back, the doctor hovering, poking, prodding, and asking dozens of questions. Once satisfied I wasn't going to bleed to death or the ribs had punctured lungs, he patted my shoulder that wasn't bruised and had me take a couple of pain pills.

"Take it easy." He glanced across the bed at Ricky who stood like a sentinel on the other side. "She needs rest—and lots of it."

"I'll stay with her tonight," Mom said, pushing close as the doctor moved to pack up his instruments.

"No." Ricky's tone didn't allow for argument, and I glanced between the two, breath held. "I'm staying. I'll take care of her."

Mom opened her mouth to argue if her frown was any indication of her thoughts, but Daddy laid his hand on her arm.

He understands.

"We're attached at the hip now, just like you and Daddy," I told her. "I'm not letting Ricky out of my sight ever again."

"That so?" Daddy's eyebrow rose as he glanced

across the bed at my man. "And when she's dancing?"

"I'll be watching, chest swelled with pride my woman is doing what she enjoys."

"And all the men around you lusting after her?"

Ricky chuckled while crossing his arms and lifting his chin. "They can look all they want and be jealous knowing she'll be in my bed every night."

"Every night, huh?"

"For the rest of her life—if she'll have me." He glanced down at me, and the emotions in his eyes slammed me in my sore chest. So much longing, but perhaps the beginnings of love, too. Warmth swirled up through my body, and I smiled through rising tears.

"Hell, yes," I whispered, unable to tear my focus off his face.

Mom kissed my cheek. "Call me if you need me, baby." Her voice whispered against my ear held resignation, but a bit of happiness as well.

I nodded, but didn't look away from Ricky. Drowning in a sea of blue, I barely took note of my parents and the doctor's departure.

"Gonna go lock up—be right back." Ricky left me alone, his fine ass hugged by dark jeans, his boots thumping on the hardwood floors.

Still smiling, I closed my eyes, my brain growing fuzzy from the meds the doctor had given me.

The bed dipped what seemed a heartbeat later, and I realized I must have dozed off.

Warm, bare skin pressed gently against my side, Ricky's hand curling around mine resting on my stomach. My eyelids refused to budge.

"I told you I could live without you," I whispered, sleep tugging at me, but I had to speak what needed put into the atmosphere to make things right. "But I don't *want* to. You're the moon in my night, Ricky, and I would be lost without you. I won't ever cling like her—"

"I don't want you to," he interrupted me. "I want *you*, Casey. I meant every word I said. You're perfection. My sunlight. My reason for breathing."

"I'm stubborn and a pain in the ass," I argued because he needed to know my weaknesses.

"I love your strength," he tossed right back.

"I've failed in so many things."

"Everyone does, baby. Look at it as an opportunity to begin again."

I smiled, the darkness behind my eyelids beckoning to me. "How did you get so smart?"

"By failing."

Such a good man... But I had more to spew. "I can get a bit rebellious when men try to control me."

"I think it's confidence in knowing you can stand on your *own* two feet."

A shuddering sigh slipped past my lips, and he pressed his against mine, breathing me in.

"I hate feeling like I'm not good enough, Ricky."

"But you are." He kissed me gently, tingling my toes. "You're everything I didn't know I wanted or needed."

Fuzziness hovered at the edge of my consciousness.

"Really gonna let your old lady continue dancing for a bunch of horny pigs?" I muttered, smiling and starting to drift off.

"They'll know your mine."

"How's that?"

"By the ink you're getting above your fine ass stating *Property of Ricky*."

I might have giggled. I definitely agreed to tattoo his name on my skin—without argument.

31

RICKY

THREE MONTHS LATER

Goddamn, I did *not* miss the cold.

Even with the rental's heater blasting on high, New England's frigid winter wind rocked the car and seemed to seep through the cracks. At least it wasn't snowing.

I stared at the Viper's club waiting in front of us, twirling my old lady's wedding band with my thumb as our hands clasped tightly atop the shifter.

"Regrets?" she asked softly, squeezing my hand.

"None." I didn't hesitate to answer—but I'd meant about every choice I'd made in life. If I hadn't gone the route I'd chosen, I wouldn't have ended up with a wedding band on my own ring finger and a tattoo on my shoulder telling the world I belonged to one Casey Lynn Capello.

Vigil hadn't made it out for our last minute Vegas wedding, but a dozen brothers had packed into the tiny chapel with us, cheers rising when I'd kissed my bride one week earlier.

I'd found my place. Fully accepted, appreciated —wanted. Needed.

I squeezed my wife's hand.

"You okay?"

I glanced over to find her soul open and vulnerable in her eyes, ready and willing to share whatever needed to be spewed in order to keep peace and help one another, same as we'd been doing for three months straight while settling into life together.

The gang that had kidnapped her turned out to be nothing more than a couple of wannabes chased out of L.A. by the real badass hoodlums. Looking for territory, they thought to take on Vegas. Stupid fuckers. Young punks whose lives ended too damn soon, no second chances, but I didn't mourn for their lives.

At least the Vipers and their loved ones were safe.

Including the ones waiting on us inside. My brothers, still my family, just extended. They would see a totally different Ricky than the one who'd left months earlier. I smiled too damn much. Enjoyed the hell out of my sober life, too. Whispers sometimes rose in my head, but having support at my right side made ignoring them a shit ton easier.

So was I okay?

Fuck, yes, but I wouldn't hold anything back from my wife.

"Demons always attack when I'm in New England, but they're quieter with you beside me." I studied the face I'd memorized from every which way, my absolute fucking favorite when she's riding my dick, her blonde hair a cascade around my head. "When I look at you, they're muffled. The past is gone. You're my future."

Her brilliant smile lit my fucking world.

"Let's go," I said, and we both hopped out of the car into the brisk wind, her curses just as loud as mine.

"Fuck, it's cold!" She clung to my hand, and I tucked her tight against my side as we hurried toward the door, the brutal wind lashing at us like a goddamn nor'easter without the wet shit.

The door wrenched open the second we drew close, Vigil grabbing me and yanking me over the threshold.

Voices hollered out greetings as the door slammed shut behind us, but I soaked in my brother's hug, his thumps on my back. "Fucking missed you."

Tears stung my eyes. "Missed you, too." No lie there, but not enough missing that I ever wanted to move back on a permanent basis.

He finally let me go, but gave me one last shoulder slap, beaming through his bushy beard, his eyes shiny with moisture. "Looking good, brother."

Another beast grabbed me, and I found myself swallowed in Ryker's hug.

Ryker. Hugging.

In my periphery, I noted Vigil lifting my girl up in a bear hug and planting a kiss on her cheek.

"The fuck got into you?" I asked Ryker with a laugh when he finally let me go.

"Had a fucking kid," Ryker grumbled, and he pulled Pia against his side, their little girl, Talia, writhing to get down. "Kinda hard to keep people out of my personal space."

"You look good, Ricky," Pia said, her cheeks a bit rounder than I'd seen her last. Motherhood looked good on her.

"Thanks."

"Oh!" Casey stepped in and held out grabby hands toward their daughter.

"She doesn't like strangers—" Pia's words cut short when her daughter reached for my woman.

"You won't be getting her back anytime soon," I warned Ryker and Pia as Casey cooed and bounced the little girl grabbing at her long waves of hair.

The introductions began.

Warden, Shaun, and their son Tyler who was only a couple weeks older than Ryker's kid stepped up next. Their brat looked just like Warden with golden skin and dark as fuck eyes.

Stone and Giada, whose belly looked ready to pop, stood behind them.

"Know what you're having?" I asked, but they shook their heads, their eyes shining with happiness I no longer coveted.

"Going to let it be a surprise," Stone said, wrapping his arms around his woman and settling his lethal hands on her belly.

Devil pushed through and yanked me in for a few back slaps, Dasia on his heels as always, stars in her eyes as she watched him.

"Bet you're not a grumpy fucker anymore now that you've got a woman worshiping the ground you walk on," he teased, stepping back with a grin. Fucker had always said nothing but a little pussy would cure my grumpiness.

I didn't tell him I got laid every damn day since Casey agreed to be mine, but I expected my own grin said enough.

Dasia's belly was flat and toned beneath her tight shirt, but I hadn't expected any different. Neither of them wanted kids. Whatever floated their boat. They sure as fucked seemed happy as hell with just the two of them in each other's lives.

Casey wanted a dozen brats—and I'd been trying to give her the first for three months straight.

Until we sat down, Casey and I with glasses of lemonade, my face hurt from smiling.

"The fucks gotten into you?" Vigil asked, grasping my shoulder before sitting down beside me.

"Happy as fuck."

"You're grinning like an idiot."

I glanced over to Mila on his other side talking to Vigil's new teenage son. Chuckling, I turned my attention back on my brother to find his grin just as wide as mine. "So are you."

"Finally slay those fucking demons of yours?" he asked, his smile fading.

"Don't know that I ever will," I admitted, my attention riveting on Casey still holding little Talia, hoping like hell I'd give her one of her own someday. "But it's easier to make the right choice when she's beside me. Lighting up my fucking life like the sun."

"Ink her name on your skin?"

"Fucking right." I pulled up the sleeve of my shirt to show off the tattoo she'd insisted on. Vigil did the same, and the similarities had us both chuckling.

I scanned the Viper's club, appreciation for each and every one of those fuckers filling me right up. We'd had a good run. They'd all had my backs—for the most part—but I definitely didn't belong there.

Casey caught my eye. *Love you*, she mouthed.

Love you more, I mouthed back my favorite line.

Her laughter sprinkled joy atop the raised voices around us.

I'd found my home where I'd never expected.

With a woman. *My* woman, a gift I sure as fuck didn't deserve but wouldn't ever complain about.

"How long you staying?" Vigil's question tore me from my musings.

"Two weeks. Casey's gotta get back to school."

"School? She decide on a different med school?"

"She decided to earn her nursing degree. Easier to do, less stress, and she can still be helping kids."

Casey had gotten into UNLV for nursing on her own, without the help of a single Viper, her daddy included. I'd never been so fucking proud of her for accepting one door had closed and another opened.

Life for me, I thought while sitting back and enjoying the Viper brotherhood, *couldn't get any better.*

Casey winked, giving me the look that let me know she had fucking on her mind—probably hoping to get knocked up seeing as how that little beauty still clung to her.

My dick twitched regardless of her reasons for wanting me, but I talked the fucker down. Okay, so maybe life at that moment could get a little better, but no way in hell we'd be getting back to our hotel anytime soon.

Casey slid onto my lap a few minutes later, right the fuck where she belonged, wrapping her arms around my neck. Her blue eyes shone with happiness, and I grinned right back, knowing I'd found my *real* home.

I'd been jealous as hell seeing my brothers have what I did in that moment—my old lady on my lap —but I no longer dealt with envy. I'd found the perfect woman, and even with all her so-called flaws she hated about herself, I fucking loved her.

"I'm going to have one of those," she said, her

whimsical voice barely registering over the ruckus, but I knew she spoke about Tyler and Talia.

"I'm trying, baby," I reminded her while squeezing her ass. "Not gonna give up until I give you what you want."

"You already did." Her eyes twinkled.

I stared, my throat working. "You serious?"

She winked, and I hoped like fuck for a little blonde girl with big blue eyes just like her momma. Two suns in my life.

Fucking right.

"Love you, baby," I choked out.

"Love you more." She pecked me on the nose.

Not fucking possible, but I wasn't about to argue with the woman who owned my heart.

THE END

ABOUT THE AUTHOR

Lynn Burke is a full-time mother, voracious gardener, and International Bestselling Author of hot romance books. A country bumpkin turned Bay Stater, she enjoys her chowdah and Dunkin Donuts when not trying to escape the reality of city life.

ALSO BY LYNN BURKE

Blood Born Series

Bonds of Worship Series

Darkest Desires Series

Dark Leopards MC

Devil's Outlaws MC

Elite Escort Series

Fallen Gliders MC

Found by Fate Series

Midnight Sun Series

Missing Link Series

Risso Family Series

Sandy Ridge Series

Vicious Vipers MC

Standalone Titles:

Abel's Obsession

Divulging Secrets

Healing Storms

In Between

The Playboy Bachelor